The Green Horse Summer

Isolde Pullum

The Green
Horse Summer

ISBN 1-933343-28-1

Stabenfeldt, Inc.
457 North Main Street
Danbury, CT 06811
www.pony.us

chapter one

"No! Please no!" Jenna screamed but the words faltered and came out as a whisper.

The water was rising, swirling and consuming her, pulling her downwards. And where was Gold? Still thrashing for his life, trapped beneath the water… Why wasn't anyone coming to save them? No breath, suffocating, drowning, help, someone, please help.

"Jenna?" Her mother's soft voice seemed to echo from a long way away. Jenna struggled in the twilight world between waking and sleeping, forcibly dragging herself back to the safety of reality and the sheltered haven of her own bedroom.

She sat up, suddenly alarmed. The room was wrong. It *wasn't* her bedroom. Where was she?

"Jenna, it's after six. You asked me to wake you. Here, I've brought you some orange juice," Angie said, looking anxiously at her only child. "Are you all right, dear? You were making some very strange noises when I came in. I hope you didn't disturb the guests."

Then it made sense. She was in one of the hotel bedrooms while her own room was being decorated. It was a gloomy, old-fashioned room, one that hadn't yet been updated and brought to life by Angie's flare for decorating. It had dark red wallpaper and old paintings in heavy frames. There was a strange collection of ornaments, vases and curios on the window sill, most of which had been taken from other rooms when they no longer fit in with the redecoration scheme. This was the third night Jenna had slept there, and the third time her dreams had taken her to a strange and terrifying place.

"I was having another horrible dream. Gold was trapped under water again, like last night, and I was drowning too. It's creepy – the night before that I was watching a ship being wrecked that you and dad were on. There was a woman standing next to me, a dark woman, watching me and crying." She shivered and sipped her orange juice. Slowly she began to feel awake and orientated and normal again.

"Poor darling, though I'm not really surprised when the last thing you see before you go to sleep is that old painting. Never mind, your room should be ready later today," Angie said as she sat on the edge of the bed and tousled her daughter's hair affectionately. "Come on, you have a lesson with Sarah this morning. You don't want to be late."

Of course! The painting, Jenna thought to herself. *I bet Mom's right*. She dressed slowly and automatically, studying the canvas in great detail. It was a crudely painted, dark, oppressive seascape with a ship tossing perilously on huge dramatic waves. Surrounded by an ornate gilt frame it was very old, part of a large collection of fixtures and fittings that had been included in the sale when her parents, Angie and Dave, had bought the Green Horse Hotel, a large, aged and rather rambling country inn.

There was something wretchedly hopeless about the ship with its broken mast and flapping sails, and for a few seconds Jenna tried to imagine what it would have been like to be on board in such a storm with no likelihood of rescue. She shivered as she remembered her dream, and with some effort she shook the dark thoughts from her mind and forcibly re-placed them with happy ones of the day ahead of her. She was booked for a jumping lesson with Gold, and, as far as Jenna was concerned, days didn't come much better than that.

"Oh help," Jenna muttered under her breath as she tried so hard to sit quietly on the anxious, sweating chestnut bounding toward a line of three solid-looking show jumps.

"Don't fiddle with your hands… and sit still!" Sarah Sheldon screamed at her, a split second before Jenna even moved a muscle, but it was enough to fix her in her saddle and allow the fences to come to meet her.

Left to his own devices, Gold flowed through the course with accuracy and flourish, even feeling confident enough to put in a little buck as they rounded the corner of the ring. Jenna, still frozen to her saddle heeding Sarah's screamed instructions, failed to take evasive action and was thrown violently to the sandy ground. Sitting up and taking stock, Jenna stared with awe at the line of fences she had just jumped. Only a few weeks ago she would never have believed she was capable. Sarah strolled over to her and offered her a hand to get up.

"I didn't mean sit still *after* the fences," she explained, smiling; "Only up to and over them – you have to ride him in-between, or he'll get away from you!"

Gold was picking at the grass that grew along the boards of the ring; veins stood out on his glossy sweat-streaked neck and his sides were heaving gently. He looked every inch the golden Thoroughbred.

"Shall we leave it there and go and have a drink? He jumped better today than I've ever seen him – you too, except for the bit at the end." Sarah was pleased with her new student. When she'd gotten the call from Harry Houseman, her celebrated ex-pupil, asking her to take Jenna on, she hadn't been sure that she wanted to. Her training days seemed far behind her and she was enjoying the less demanding life of boarding horses and trekking and teaching groups of children how to ride. It wasn't as glamorous as training ambitious young show jumpers, but it wasn't as stressful either. At her age that counted for something.

Harry Houseman had been her greatest success and was a household name now, having won a gold medal in the World Equestrian Games. Harry had met Jenna when she'd won a week of training sessions with him, as a prize in a show jumping competition. In Jenna and Gold he'd seen a partnership with promise, and he'd been touched by Jenna's determination to improve. As Jenna lived near Sarah, he'd thought an introduction might benefit both of them.

"Have you heard from Harry recently?" Jenna asked as she sat at Sarah's large, cluttered kitchen table sipping hot cocoa.

"I had an email from him a few days ago. He's in Holland competing, and doing rather well, by the sound of it. He deserves to succeed. He works hard at it."

"He certainly worked me very hard when I was with him," Jenna said, remembering with pleasure the blissful week she had spent at the Houseman stables, living and breathing horses and show jumping. The long days had gone by in a flash and the nights had passed in the deepest, most satisfying sleep she could ever remember. "I'd rather muck out a hundred stables a day than make beds and clean bathrooms at the hotel," she told Sarah, knowing she'd agree.

"Me too! How is business at your place?"

"Pretty good, I think. At least Dad hasn't been moaning about it too much. I still have to wait on tables three nights a week and help with the breakfasts, but he's taken on more staff for the weekends."

"I've been meaning to phone him about an idea I've had

to offer vacations to people who want to bring their own horses to ride in our lovely countryside. I often get asked, and although I can offer first class boarding facilities and an experienced mounted guide, they usually want luxury hotel accommodations included in the package. I don't want to get involved with having people stay here… for a start, I'd have to wash dishes properly, instead of putting them down for the dogs!"

Jenna giggled and nervously looked at her cocoa cup, hoping Sarah was joking.

"But, if I could work something out with your father, offering it as a joint venture, the guests would get the best of both worlds. Do you think it would work?" Sarah chewed thoughtfully on a grubby, battered thumbnail.

"It might. We have guests occasionally who tell me about their horses and how they'd love to ride them around here. I always feel a bit mean not offering them rides on Gold, but he really isn't quiet enough for most people."

"Do you think your dad would be interested? I've got the stabling and the local knowledge, but I can't even offer bed and breakfast here," she waved a hand around the kitchen, "not without doing housework."

Sarah shivered at the thought and Jenna smiled. Sarah's stables were tidier, better organized and probably cleaner than her kitchen, but it was a comfortable, relaxed sort of muddle, and Jenna felt welcome there.

"You can ask him. He's always looking for ways to attract more customers and make more money. Speaking of which, I'd better be going. I promised Mom I'd help her this afternoon."

Jenna left the cool darkness of the kitchen and stepped outside into blazing sunshine that made her eyes hurt. Sarah's house, a converted hay barn, made up one side of the square yard; the other three sides were lined with horse trailers, storage and an office. The pavement was gray and pitted in places, patterned with hoof marks sunk into the surface on hot days such as this one. She sat on a bench by the front door, pulled on her boots and tried to remember where she'd left her hat. Gold was tied to a post in the cool shelter of a young willow tree, planted by Sarah for that very purpose. He had emptied the hay net Jenna had left him and was almost asleep; with his bottom lip drooping and a hind leg rested, he looked relaxed and contented.

"Wake up," Jenna tightened his girth and Gold came alive with a start, knocking her hat from the post where Jenna had left it.

"Thanks, I was wondering where that was," she said as she brushed the dust off it and fastened it onto her head.

For most of the next thirty minutes as she rode home she was thinking about Sarah's proposal, and what it might mean to her if the hotel suddenly became full of horsy people. Perhaps she would be allowed to go out on some of the rides with them, maybe even guide them herself if Sarah was too busy. Perhaps James could come too, when he was around. Jenna's heart leaped a little as she thought about James. James was her boyfriend, and although he lived a long way away, he had recently learned to drive and was allowed to borrow his mom's car so he could come to see Jenna more often. He was tall and fair, good-looking in a very regular way. Lots of girls chased after him, but he only had eyes for Jenna. This was possibly because, at first, Jenna had had her sights set on someone else and had hardly noticed James. He'd had to work very hard to win her over. That someone else was Steve, dark-haired, dangerously handsome and several years too old for Jenna. He rented the stable yard at the Green Horse Hotel, and he was trying to make a name for himself as a racehorse trainer. He adored Jenna as he would have adored a little sister had he had one, though on more than one occasion he found himself wishing she were nearer his age and not going out with James. Jenna adored Steve too, with a wistful, hopeless longing for someone unobtainable. She thought of it as a teenage crush, and she thought she had gotten in under control, but there were times when a look passed between them that reignited a dangerously enchanting flame within her heart. From the time they had first met he had trusted her with his precious horses and believed in her dreams about becoming a professional show jumper. It was Steve who had brought Gold to the Green Horse Hotel, and it was Steve who had taught her to ride him. Jenna felt that she owed him a great deal.

Tufty whinnied to Gold as they passed his paddock. The old pony had been at the hotel for as long as anyone in the village could remember, and he was the first pony that Jenna had ever properly called her own. She loved him dearly. He was ancient, his muzzle gray and his paces stiff and shuffling, but he still seemed happy pottering around the field and eating the sweet summer grasses.

When Jenna rode into the yard, she thought, as she always did, how beautiful the tattered old stables were. Built at the same time as the hotel, but boarded up until recently, the stone was rich in color and the little leaded windows seemed to be blinking short-sightedly in a friendly, elderly way. The arched doors into the central stall area were open and Jenna could hear Steve singing along to the radio as he did his paperwork in the tack-room that he also used as an office. Against Jenna's wishes, her heart did its familiar little leap again, this time at the thought of Steve. Jenna knew she wasn't completely over him, despite her strong feelings for James. Hearing hoof beats, Steve came into the yard, welcoming any excuse to stop the boredom he always felt when he sat at a desk and tried to make sense of figures and forms and writing letters.

"Hi, how did the lesson go?" He smiled at Jenna and held Gold for her while she dismounted.

"Good, thanks. I only fell off once and Gold jumped beautifully. Sarah's really nice. Have you met her?"

"No, but I'd like to, I've heard a lot about her over the years. I think dad knows her."

"Do you know what the time is?" Jenna shook her watch but the hands refused to move.

"Half past three. Your Mom came down a few minutes ago looking for you."

"Oh, no! I'm supposed to be helping her. I didn't realize it was so late."

"I'll feed Gold for you and you can run along," Steve placed a friendly hand on her shoulder.

"Would you? Thanks, I'd better run."

Absentmindedly, Steve rubbed Gold behind his ear, as he watched Jenna race from the yard, stripping hat and gloves and sweatshirt as she ran. Gold gave a little sigh and shut his eyes, reveling in the delicious scratching of a spot impossible to reach when you only have hooves. He was warm and tired after his work and his mind went longingly to his stall, which was prepared for him, perhaps with feed in the box, certainly with a net full of sweet, dry hay. He nudged Steve out of his daydream and together they walked into the cool darkness of the stables.

"Sorry, my watch stopped," Jenna flew into the kitchen, half undressed, on her way to change.

"Oh there you are, Jen. I was wondering where you'd gone. Can you start peeling these potatoes and I'll get the carrots washed." Her mother seemed a bit flustered, as she

12

often was at the beginning of a busy evening working in the kitchen.

"That's not a very original excuse," her dad remarked. He was counting cutlery and crockery in front of a large, metal storage cupboard, and making notes on a clipboard.

"It's true though, look," she waved her wrist under his nose.

"Pooh, you smell of stables! Go and wash. I'll start peeling the potatoes for you, but hurry up or I'll dock your wages!"

"Thanks, dad," Jenna kissed him on the cheek as she passed.

Arriving back in the kitchen ten minutes later, this time smelling of grapefruit soap and toothpaste, Jenna took over the potato peeler from her father and was disappointed to discover just four small spheres shining whitely from the bottom of the stainless steel bowl.

"I've just been speaking to your friend Sarah on the phone," Dave Wells told his daughter. "She's got this idea for offering upscale guided treks and wants us to go in with her. Your mom and I were just discussing it before you came in."

Jenna stopped, mid potato, to look at her father.

"Are we going to do it? I think it's a brilliant idea. Sarah was telling me about it after the lesson."

"Don't you think people would rather have the hotel a bit closer to where their horses are stabled?" Dave asked.

"It's only ten minutes by car," Angie said, not even looking up from the cream she was piping onto a large, exotic fruit trifle, "and they might be glad to get away from them by the evenings."

"What are Sarah's facilities like, Jenna?" Dave asked.

"Oh, her stables are quite old but very tidy; she has a big sand school with jumps, but I imagine the people she's trying to attract are more interested in trail riding than jumping."

"How many spare stalls do we have down in our stables?"

"Well, none that are fit to be used; the four next to Tufty's stable are full of old furniture and the doors are wrecked on most of them," said Jenna, wondering where this conversation was going.

"It wouldn't take much to clear them out and get some new doors, would it? Why shouldn't *we* offer the complete package here? Jenna could be groom and guide. You're always saying you prefer mucking out and feeding horses to mucking out and feeding people. It needn't be a big deal; just another facility we can offer our guests."

For a few seconds Jenna thrilled to this new idea, but then she remembered Sarah.

"It was Sarah's idea. It would be too mean to just steal it from her," she looked earnestly at her father.

"Well, it's not exactly original. I've heard of other hotels doing it. Anyway, business is business. You can't afford to have too many scruples in the hotel game."

"But Dad, you *can't* do it, Sarah's my friend. How can I face her and go on having lessons with her if you stab her in the back like this?" Jenna was shocked by what she saw as her father's lack of principles.

"Jenna, Sarah won't see it like that, and if she's any sort of businesswoman she won't turn away lessons. Not that you'll have much time for them if you're going to be looking after the guests' horses." Dave Wells saw most things in a very black and white way, unlike his wife and his daughter.

"It really wouldn't be kind, Dave," Angie said, stopping her work to gaze at him, mulling over the stubborn side of his nature. Jenna really should know better than to tell him *not* to do something. It was the surest way to make him do it.

"I haven't decided what to do yet," Dave said crossly; he hated being criticized by Jenna, especially when all he was trying to do was to make a good living for his family. He played his trump card, which, he knew from long experience, always got Jenna off her high horse. "Whatever my decision is, may I remind you, young lady, that we are running a business here? And if it doesn't succeed, we'll all be going back to London to live."

Jenna said nothing and kept her angry, tear-filled eyes down. She went back to peeling potatoes and stifled the urge to throw one at her father's broad back as he left through the kitchen door.

Dave Wells walked thoughtfully through the kitchen garden to the stable yard, a place he rarely visited. Such was the pace of hotel life during the summer months. The faded elegance of the old stone building struck him, and the warm sunshine brought out the smell of straw and horse and summer grasses, which he found strangely calming for its earthiness and closeness to the natural world he had mostly lost touch with. He knew he was alone because Steve's sports car was missing from its usual parking place. Well, perhaps not quite alone, he thought to himself, as four pairs of eyes watched him curiously from various parts of the yard. Steve's horses, Giselle and Flash Harry, looked tall and rather snooty, Dave thought, and Tufty was wearing his bored expression, which stated quite clearly that he'd rather be left alone. Dave went over to Gold and patted him inexpertly and rather too firmly on his long, delicate nose, causing the chestnut to fling his head up in surprise.

"Sorry, old man," Dave muttered, amused to find himself talking to a horse. He tried again, this time more gently, and was rewarded when Gold lowered his head and sighed in appreciation.

Dave looked in the old stables, which were piled high with

15

stored furniture and boxes of documents taken from the hotel offices when they'd first moved in. He assessed the work that would need to be done and came up with a figure he could easily realize within a few good weeks of bookings.

"I think you may find that things will start to liven up a bit around here," he told Gold as he passed him again on his way back to the hotel.

That night Jenna was back in her own bedroom which was now a pretty shade of blue with new, patterned blinds and a luxurious, deep-pile carpet. It was stylish but impersonal because, as yet, there was nothing familiar in it. There was also a strong smell of fresh paint, but Jenna hardly noticed any of this, so angry was she with her father. She threw herself into bed and tossed and turned for over an hour until exhaustion overcame her and she slept, deeply and without dreaming, for the first time in three days.

chapter two

It took Dave just a few days to arrange for the stables to be cleared and made habitable, and even less time for the new idea for the horse riding vacations to be put on the Green Horse Hotel website. With characteristic enterprise, he contacted a journalist friend who knew a man, who knew a woman who could get an article written about the new venture in the prestigious weekly magazine, HORSE.

It took slightly longer for Jenna to forgive him, if indeed she really did, but she learned to accept what seemed to be inevitable, and on some level she was pleased with the plans.

Sarah wasn't. She called Dave all the names she could think of, none of which was the least bit flattering, and stated quite bluntly that she was no longer prepared to coach Jenna and Gold.

"So, that's my show-jumping career over before it even started," Jenna moaned to James when he came to see her compete at a small local show.

"There are other coaches," he told her.

"Not as good as Sarah, and not around here there aren't. And not ones personally recommended by Harry Houseman. It feels as though I'm letting him down as much as anything." Jenna was determined not to be cheered up. "I just can't understand my dad sometimes."

"Maybe one of the guests will turn out to be a famous

show jumper and give you lessons," James was snatching at straws now, but he hated it when Jenna was down.

"Oh, get real! They'll be ancient pony trekkers festooned with saddlebags and water bottles who never go faster than a trot! And they'll lag miles behind Gold and 'tut tut' at me if any of their horses raises a sweat!"

James laughed at her and put his arm around her shoulder in a very understanding way, which made Jenna feel a little more human.

She was tired. She had gotten up very early to groom and braid Gold and to ride the six miles to the showground – a gently sloping field that had recently been grazed by cows. The first class, for riders under sixteen, had finished before James had arrived, and although Jenna had won it easily she felt no real sense of achievement as she led the gallop around the arena. The class she really wanted to do well in was taking place after lunch, and in that she would be up against experienced adults, riding established horses. Jenna was far from experienced and Gold's jumping was certainly not established, but between them they had a huge amount of courage and a depth of understanding that most horse and rider partnerships only ever dreamed of.

James took his self-appointed role of Jenna's groom and general guardian seriously. Leaving her to watch the other competitors, he went in search of a sugar-laden energy drink to go with the bananas he had brought with him as part of their picnic lunch. On returning, he sat her down to eat and drink while he brushed Gold's chestnut coat and put extra chalk on his white markings. Gold's socks and blaze were dazzling in the sunlight, which also picked out all the sparkles in his rich, red-gold summer color. He was a most satisfying horse to groom, thought James, when very little effort with a body brush could do so much. Not like his

18

Mom's horse, Charlie, whose gray coat never really shone no matter how hard you worked on it.

Jenna was very focused watching the other riders perform, and she was oblivious to the giggling of a small group of teenage girls who were smiling at James, trying to get him to notice them. What did Jenna have, they asked themselves, to get a gorgeous guy like James running around after her? She didn't even seem grateful!

"Time you were warming up, Jen." James brought Gold to her and waited while she fastened her hat before legging her easily into the saddle.

"Thanks. Can you come and put the practice jump up, please?" Her words were flat and she found she couldn't smile now that the start of her round approached and set her nerves jangling.

Luckily, James understood, but the group of girls, all of whom wore make-up and the latest styles of riding jacket, stared open-mouthed at Jenna and wondered how she did it.

The practice ring was crowded and Jenna suddenly felt very young as she realized that all the other riders were years older than she. James took his life in his hands as he ran across the ring, dodging wound-up, overexcited horses to get to the two practice fences in the middle. He went to lower one, but was shouted at by a plump man on a steel gray horse who thundered over the fence, knocking the top pole flying as he went.

James replaced the pole and looked for Jenna who was struggling with Gold, doing her best to keep him relaxed and calm, but failing miserably as each passing horse reminded him of his racing background when he had been in training with Steve.

"Maybe it would be better not to warm up here, with all the other horses," James suggested when she passed near enough to hear him.

19

Jenna nodded and trotted Gold toward the trailers. James followed, glad to be clear of the flying hooves and the tense, nervous riders.

Away from the other horses, Gold settled down quickly and began to soften his jaw and stretch his back when Jenna asked him to with her seat and her legs and her reins. He wore a bitless bridle, which was the only thing Jenna had found he was comfortable with; it had been her discovery of this that had been a breakthrough in their relationship together. It worked well for them, and Gold respected and accepted Jenna's contact through the reins without fighting her. She worked him at trot and canter for a few minutes before she was satisfied that her horse was now relaxed enough and his muscles warmed up sufficiently for them to tackle the show-jumping round ahead of them.

"I don't think I dare take him back into the practice ring," she told James. "Do you think it will be all right to go straight in without jumping him?" he asked her. "We were always taught not to at the Pony Club."

"It will have to be. Oh, I wish Steve were here. He'd know how to advise me." Her words were out before she realized what she'd said and she looked at James, trying to gauge his reactions, but he'd turned away and she didn't see the look of disappointment that ghosted across his kind, handsome face. He was used to feeling second best to Steve, but it didn't mean that he liked being reminded that he was only the substitute.

"Sarah's over there," James had noticed her talking to an elderly couple sitting on picnic chairs at the ringside. "Do you want me to get her?"

Jenna nodded weakly. She had never felt so nervous before. Her mouth was dry, and she felt so weak she could hardly muster the energy to keep Gold walking around in circles.

Jenna was too far away to hear the conversation that took place between James and Sarah, but it wasn't hard to guess roughly what had been said. James returned, his face burning with embarrassment and anger.

"She says she's too busy and she's not in the habit of giving free advice… sorry, Jen."

Sarah's rebuff had a strangely positive affect on Jenna. It wasn't that she blamed her – she was as angry with her father as Sarah must have been – but she had never been able to understand why adults sometimes behaved like children, doing all the things themselves that they were forever telling young people not to. Jenna was used to sorting herself out – all her life her parents, though supportive from a distance, had been too busy to be involved with her dreams and ambitions. Without meaning to, they had created in Jenna a rare independence, which kicked in now. She rode Gold away and found a quiet space where she practiced leg yielding and turns on the forehand, rein-back and walk-to-canter transitions. These were all movements that Steve had taught them to do as a way of making Gold supple and obedient and, most important, making him concentrate on Jenna instead of worrying about what was going on around him.

The question as to how wise it was not to do a practice fence was suddenly taken out of her hands when she heard her number being called by the announcer. She cantered Gold over to where he stood, flustered, hot, harassed and wondering why he was giving up his day off from being a taxi-driver to stand in a field shouting at overwrought competitors on wound-up horses. Somehow it didn't seem fair. And here was another one, galloping her great horse far too close to him and not looking as if she was enjoying herself one little bit. He noticed Jenna's frightened eyes and softened a little.

She looked so young compared to the other competitors in this class... and pretty, too!

"You're in next, hon," he told her, "gorgeous horse you've got."

Jenna looked down at him and smiled, "Thank you. He's still young."

Jenna and Gold trotted into the ring as the last competitor left it. The fences were plastic and Jenna thought that they didn't look as big from the back of her brave horse as they had when she had walked the course on foot. She asked Gold to canter and he picked up speed obediently as they headed for the first fence, the starting bell ringing in their ears.

"Sit still! Sit still!" Jenna told herself as she tried to trust that Gold's approach would be steady. It was. Between them they managed to keep each other calm and, as fence after fence disappeared beneath them without a pole dropping, Jenna's smile broadened as she realized how much she was loving every precious second.

"Clear round for Jenna Wells and Gold," said the loud-speaker.

Jenna jumped down from Gold and hugged James, making up for the quiet, pre-competition surliness brought on by her nerves.

"That looked easy – he was jumping out of his skin," James told her, still holding her close to him.

"He felt amazing, and he was listening to me all the way around – it was as if I had four legs and wings!" Jenna's face was flushed with excitement and effort.

"Have you learned the jump-off course?" James asked.

"Yes, that was one of the things that Harry Houseman drummed into us – always check out the jump-off when you walk the course, because you won't get the chance later."

"At Pony Club I never learned the jump-off course, because

I always thought it was tempting fate too much – as if I was assuming that I'd get a clear round, which I hardly ever did because Charlie always knocked a pole down," James remembered.

"Harry always taught us to be positive – so of course we'd need to know the jump-off!" Jenna told him, grinning from ear to ear.

There were several clear rounds in Jenna's class, which was proving to be a well-contested competition, full of good horses and riders. Jenna had a whole hour in which to get nervous again before her number was called and she entered the ring for the second round. This time speed was important, but not in the way that Gold, as an ex-racehorse, was inclined to see it. Jenna knew from bitter experience that if she asked Gold to gallop, his jumping would suffer as his stride became longer and flatter. What she needed to do was to cut corners and jump at sharp angles to shave the seconds off her time, and it was something she had practiced and become quite good at, but she had to have Gold's attention one hundred percent to succeed. She circled at a canter while the ring crew rebuilt a fence that the last competitor had demolished.

"Hurry up," she muttered under her breath, as her nervousness began to communicate itself to Gold.

At last the bell rang and Gold sprang forward toward the first fence, which was a stark rustic upright. He popped over neatly, and as he was landing Jenna leaned her weight left, lining him up to nip inside a fence and find a new line to a big spread which was now the second fence. Coming upon it rather suddenly, Gold had to find an extra leg to get over it, but it stayed up and on they went, each angle getting sharper and more daring as Jenna tested her horse's powers to the extreme over the large, imposing fences. People at the ringside stopped talking to stare at the young girl and her lovely chestnut horse, willing the fences to stay up as they flew over them at seemingly impossible angles. At the very last, their luck ran out and Gold's hoof just toppled the back rail. There was a disappointed groan from the crowd and some sighs of relief from the waiting, mounted competitors in the collecting ring.

James ran to Jenna, expecting her to be disappointed, but he found her hugging Gold happily and feeding him mints, which he loved.

"You'll be the fastest four faults and there's only been one clear round so far," he told her.

"I don't care about winning," she told him, "not today anyway. I'm just so thrilled with the way he jumped. It was amazing! He tried so hard for me. I just love him so much, James! Where's my phone? I should send Steve a text message."

"Here, borrow mine," James said, handing her his expensive, state-of-the-art phone. "And while you're at it, send him my love," he added, but not loud enough for Jenna to hear.

chapter three

"No more shows for a bit, Jenna," Dave Wells told his daughter firmly, after he'd listened to the account of Gold's supersonic round, and eventual third place, for the fifth time. "We've got a couple bringing their horses at the end of the week, and you haven't worked out the rides for them yet."

"I'll do it tomorrow," she promised. Then she had a thought. "Do I get paid for researching the routes, or just for being an escort?"

"Don't push your luck, young lady, or I might start charging you for Gold's stabling and feed," he said with mock firmness. But he patted her shoulder affectionately as he left the kitchen, summoned by the little hand-bell that was left at reception.

"Try this, Jen," Angie put a dish in front of her daughter, "it's peach tart. It's going on the menu tonight for the first time – do you think it's good enough?"

The mixture of sweet fruit and caramelized, juice-soaked pastry was blissful, and Jenna told her mother so by rolling her eyes heavenward and making appreciative noises, as her mouth was too full to answer more specifically or politely.

"I'll take that as a yes, then," said Angie, "If there's any left, I'll wrap a piece up in foil and put it in your lunch tomorrow."

"There won't be. Once word gets round the restaurant, everyone will be ordering it," said Jenna. "Maybe I'd better have another piece now, just to make sure it really is good enough for our guests!"

Jenna left for her ride early the next morning while the day was still relatively cool. She sat tall on Gold, and Steve watched her as she set off down the drive. Part of him would have loved to go with her. She was such good company and fun to be with, and he wasn't quite sure what was stopping him. He didn't have anything to do that day which couldn't wait a little longer – it was just that he was very aware of how Jenna felt about him and he didn't want to encourage her. But did that really matter now that she was so obviously firmly established as James's girlfriend? He sighed and went back to his mucking out.

Gold's long, loose stride ate up the country lanes, and soon Jenna was crossing the main road (quiet at this time of the morning) and trotting along a bridle path that crossed some high land with stunning views across to the coast. Jenna was sure that the guests at the Green Horse Hotel couldn't fail to be impressed by the scenery here. The bridle path had once been a tramline that linked one side of the county to the other, and used to carry stone away from the quarries that had been worked there. Now unused, the holes had filled with water and become lakes, the home of frogs, newts, fish and insects, and the haunt of local fishermen. Jenna stopped at one and walked Gold over the gravel shoreline so that he could wade up to his knees. He snorted and plunged his muzzle deep into the cold water and started to paw the ground, sending up silver cascades that showered over Jenna and soaked the legs of her jodhpurs. She looked down at the water as it churned brown and white in waves that traveled toward the quarry edge then bounced back at them, making Gold snort in surprise, though he didn't cease his frenzied splashing.

"Hey, stop it," Jenna laughed, her face dripping, but she didn't really mind. He was so obviously enjoying himself and the day was hot enough to make the experience rather pleasant. Jenna rode reluctantly away when she realized she was being glared at by some fishermen who weren't impressed by Gold stirring up the water and disturbing the fish.

The path was mostly stony, but for some of the way there was a wide grassy verge, and she let Gold canter along it, reveling in the feeling of her long-striding, well-balanced horse and loving him with all her heart for his magnificence and boldness. They trotted and cantered along lanes and tracks nearly all the way to the coast, and then Jenna pulled up and walked more carefully along the path, which wound its way rather near to the edge of the steeply plummeting cliff. Recent savage storms had eroded the track, and Gold stepped nervously on the fresh-looking subsoil. The tide was turning and, although still early, the far side of the beach was already becoming crowded with colorful little huddles of tents, windbreaks and people sitting on towels and deckchairs. The near side was empty; a large sign warning about treacherous quicksand was enough to keep people away. Distracted, Gold strode on, watching the sea and the surfers and not looking where his feet were going. Twice he tripped and Jenna spoke to him sharply, fearful of the drop. Suddenly her eyes were arrested by something strange; familiar enough in another place, but frighteningly out of context. Halting Gold, she stared down at the shallow water just beyond the turn of the tide, and tried to make sense of what she saw. It appeared to be a horse's head jutting through the sand bed as if trapped beneath and struggling to rise, though there was no movement except the gentle wavelets and the sun's bright reflection dancing on the water. Jenna was too far away to be sure of anything, and she wished she had brought her father's binoculars with her. As the water got slowly deeper, the horse disappeared from sight, leaving Jenna with doubt in her mind as to what she had seen. Was it just a strangely shaped rock? Could it have been a real horse? It reminded her, rather disturbingly, of her nightmares. There was *something* real about it, but not flesh and blood real, she thought to herself as she turned slowly away and made for the busy end of the bay, where she knew she could get herself an ice cream cone.

The sun was almost overhead by the time Jenna reached the little stand. There was a long line of hot-looking adults and excited, noisy children. They turned and looked at Gold and Jenna when they heard his hooves, heavy on the thick dune grass. Jenna jumped down and asked a friendly-looking man at the end of the line if he would mind getting her a large strawberry cone with chocolate sprinkles if she gave him the money, and she explained that Gold found it difficult to stand in an orderly line as he couldn't help fidgeting. The man smiled and agreed, and Jenna took Gold to a patch of grass and let him pick at it, which he did with such enthusiasm that Jenna was embarrassed in case someone should think she didn't feed him properly. A small girl left her father's side and came shyly up to pat Gold, who stopped eating long enough to accept an offered peppermint from the child's hot, grimy hand. Jenna recognized the look of pure pleasure in the girl's eyes as Gold's lips gently took the mint and then stood and allowed her to rub his cheek for a few seconds, as his large teeth crunched the tiny sweet.

"Here you are, hon," the kind-looking man said as he handed Jenna a large, dripping ice cream cone and some change. "Eat it quickly, or it will melt."

Jenna thanked him and did as she was told, sharing the last drips with two wasps who seemed as keen on ice cream as she.

When she'd finished, Jenna studied the map she had brought with her and checked her route for the afternoon. It would take them inland, away from the coast, to some wooded areas that Jenna had not ridden through before. She set off again, feeling a little intrepid and a little lonely, wishing that she had someone to talk to and share the adventure with. James was working at a bookshop during the summer vacation, and when she'd asked Steve to come with her, he'd made up some excuse about waiting for a phone call, which was pretty silly because he always used a cell phone. She was aware that Steve sometimes felt awkward about their friendship and she was slightly amused by it, liking the effect she could sometimes have on him with just a look. But it sometimes made her sad too, because although she had let go of the idea that there could be a relationship between them because of the difference in their ages, she was aware of a special kind of magic that passed between them from time to time. It wasn't there with James, fond of him though she was.

Gold's hooves made a steady rhythm on the pavement as they left the dunes and turned down a quiet lane that ran beside a stream. Jenna found a place where Gold could walk into the water and he drank deeply before beginning his splashing games again.

"Come on you, we haven't got time for this now. This is supposed to be a four hour trail ride, and we've taken three already!" she chided him.

If he could have answered, Gold might have pointed out that it was Jenna who had stopped for ice cream, not he, and Jenna who had waited on the cliffs for a full ten minutes staring vacantly out to sea!

The trees overhead made the lane dark and cool and Jenna asked Gold to trot, enjoying his swinging stride as the time slipped past. Eventually she found the entrance to the woods, marked with a post and arrow as a bridle path. It was soft underfoot, and Gold galloped strongly up the gentle incline, sensing he had turned for home, with thoughts of hay nets and buckets of feed spurring him on and erasing his tiredness. The hill became steeper, and at the top the trees cleared and Jenna found a spectacular panoramic view stretching out before her. In the distance she recognized the steeple of the church in her village and knew she wasn't far from home, but it was another half hour before she found herself riding up through the main village street, hot, weary and ready for a cold drink. As always, Mr. Penrose was in his garden as she passed.

"Been far?" he called.

"Miles!" she answered. "Planning routes for the riding guests. I've been to Rush Bay today and back through Redmoor woods. Have you got any ideas for places I can take them?"

"Have you thought about Pendle Mount? There are some standing stones there worth seeing, and if you take them up on Horse Hill they'll be able to see both coasts at the same time – providing it's a clear day." The old man looked down at his feet, "Been to Rush Bay, have you? I haven't been there for years. It *is* very beautiful, but keep the horses on the far side of the bay. Those sands can be treacherous."

"That reminds me, when I was on the cliff path at Rush I thought I saw a something under the water. It was really weird. It looked like a horse's head, not real I don't think, more like a statue or something, but I suppose it must have been a rock, or the light playing funny tricks."

Mr. Penrose gave a little gasp.

"Are you all right?" Jenna asked anxiously.

The old man looked startled, and he leaned against the

gate for support. His face was pale and he had a faraway expression in his watery old eyes.

"Are you all right?" Jenna asked again.

Mr. Penrose nodded and Jenna was relieved to see the color returning to his worn, wrinkled face.

"I think so, dear. It's just that what you said made me feel a bit odd, because I saw that horse too, a very long time ago."

"How strange! I wonder what it is." Jenna had doubted herself up to this point.

"At first I thought it was a real horse, in trouble in the sinking sands. It was the morning after some really bad storms and there had been quite a bit of damage done in the area, trees blown over and several fences down. Some cattle had escaped on to the dunes and I was helping to round them up when I saw it." Mr. Penrose rubbed his hand over his forehead thoughtfully and his old eyes stared into the far distance. "I saw a horse's head, just like you said, though it was gone on the next tide and no one would believe me. Just said I was a silly fool who needed to see an optician – or a psychiatrist, though they didn't quite have the nerve to say *that* to my face, but it was certainly what they thought!"

"What do you suppose it is?" Jenna wondered.

"Whatever it is, you'd be well advised to forget about it. Don't meddle with what you don't understand and then you'll come to no harm," Mr. Penrose turned and stomped off up his garden, leaving the conversation unsatisfactorily unfinished.

"Give my regards to your parents," he called back to her as he closed his front door behind him.

31

chapter four

"He was his usual cagey, 'don't mess with the supernatural' self," Jenna informed her mother, in between gulps of cold water taken straight from the kitchen tap.

"Why can't you use a glass like a normal person, or are you turning into a horse?"

"Sorry, I was desperate for a drink! I forgot to take water with me on the ride. What do think the horse could be? The more I think about it, the more it reminded me of a statue, though what on earth a statue would be doing under the water I can't begin to imagine. Mr. Penrose seemed to be suggesting it was some kind of apparition; he's so superstitious and he's frightened of anything he doesn't understand. Can you remember how jumpy he was when we were doing the research for the murder mystery plot and all that stuff came up about the brothers' feud? He kept saying no good would come of it."

"Yes," said Angie thoughtfully, "and I also remember that he was proved right, partly."

Jenna looked at a large, red scar on the palm of her right hand, which would remain with her forever, after a pistol she had found in an ancient tin box had gone off as she held it.

"Hmm. Well, I'm not sure what I saw, but if he's seen it too, then that must surely prove there's something there. I wonder if we could borrow a boat and have a look sometime."

"Why not ask Sheila about it? She'll be up to work later.

See what she has to say before you get too excited," her mother advised.

Sheila was the plump, homely, middle-aged daughter of Mr. Penrose. She was his fiercest supporter and his greatest critic, having grown up and grown tired of his stories long ago, and was the first to dismiss them as nonsense. She worked part-time as a waitress in the Green Horse restaurant and was almost as good a source of local information and gossip as was her elderly father.

Yes, thought Jenna, as she took a plate with a large slice of her mother's fruitcake to the lounge in the private part of the hotel. Yes, Sheila would be the best person to ask. She turned the TV on, and sank down into a large, saggy armchair that seemed to wrap itself around her as she started on the cake.

The next morning Jenna was down at the stables early again, with a packed lunch, a small bottle of water and her father's binoculars to stuff into her saddlebag. She called to Gold as she went through the arched doorway and was rewarded when he called back to her with a low, snuffling nicker as he asked for his breakfast.

"Feed Giselle for me, Jen. Harry's already had his," Steve called from the tack room.

"OK," she replied.

In the feed store she found two buckets, and into each one she mixed sugar beet, wet and sweet smelling, with a scoop of mixed food, a little salt and some vegetable oil. When the horses saw her coming, both called urgently to her and kicked at their doors impatiently. Jenna fed Giselle first because the mare could never wait for anything, especially food. Gold was just as eager, but he was naturally more polite and he stood back from the door as Jenna entered his stable and tipped the contents of the bucket into his feeder. It was an old cast iron feeder with a rolled top and a pale blue tiled ring, which contrasted with the rich brown, mahogany paneling. The stalls were rather grand, though very old, dating back to the days when the Green Horse Hotel had been a busy coaching inn catering to wealthy travelers and their horses. Gold was unimpressed by the history of his home, though not completely untouched by it. Sometimes, on very dark, quiet nights he could feel the presence of past occupants, both equine and human, and though he was a little confused by them, he was a brave, self-assured young horse and they did not worry him unduly.

Happy just to be with him, Jenna watched him eat, amused at the way he picked up one foreleg and pawed the air with engrossed enjoyment of his food. She started to groom the silky coat, polishing the hair with firm strokes of a soft body brush.

"Where are you going today?" Steve asked her.

"Pendle Mount, then back home over Horse Hill. I need some idea of how long it will take and I want to know if the people who run the café on the bike path mind horses being tied up outside. They didn't used to, but Dad says it would be best to ask before I take guests there." Jenna didn't look up from her grooming but she could sense Steve's eyes on her.

"Mind if Giselle and I join you?" he asked lightly.

"If you think you can keep up with me," Jenna answered with a delighted grin. She'd been happy before at the thought of a day in Gold's company, but the addition of Steve would make it perfect. She sang to herself as she started on the heavy, pungent task of mucking out.

An hour later they were both mounted. Steve wore jeans and short boots, a white tee shirt and a battered skullcap without a silk cover. He looked raffish and wild, in need of a haircut,

34

but arrestingly handsome as he sat lightly, his long legs doubled up into the diminutive leathers of the racing saddle. It would have been agonizing for Jenna to ride with her stirrups so short, but Steve had been doing it since he was a small boy at his father's training yard, and to him it felt as natural as walking.

Jenna looked slight and rather waif-like in old blue jodhpurs, faded and patched, and a striped, sleeveless tee shirt that showed off her tanned, lightly-muscled arms and shoulders. Beneath her Gold looked huge, leggy and magnificent, Steve thought affectionately. He always had been his favorite horse, and he was glad that Jenna had him now and obviously loved him so much. They left the yard side by side and rode without speaking along the quiet lanes in the cool of the early morning, both content with their lot and happy with their own silent thoughts.

Jenna wondered what Steve was thinking. It was impossible to tell, as he wasn't the sort to let his feelings show. Jenna's own thoughts went back to the mysterious Sand Horse, which was the name she now gave to it after the conversation she had had with Sheila in the kitchen the evening before.

"Oh, the silly old fool, he's not going on about that sand horse again, is he?" she had asked in her loud, good-natured voice.

When Jenna had explained that she had also seen the horse, Sheila's eyes narrowed as she considered what the boss's daughter had just told her. It was one thing to doubt the sanity of your own father, but perhaps she'd better be careful what she said about Jenna if she wanted to maintain the good relationship she had with her employers.

"Well, maybe he did see *something*, and maybe *you* did too, but at least *you* weren't foolish enough to think it was real and go to rescue it like he did."

35

"It did cross my mind that it *might* be a real horse, but only for a second. Why, what did your dad do?" Jenna asked.

"He climbed down to the beach and waded out to where he thought he'd seen it. It was almost dark too, but he didn't stop to think about that. He was up to his waist in water when he fell into a great patch of quicksand – the only thing that saved him was that the tide was rising so quickly and he was able to keep calm until he was afloat. Mom didn't speak to him for a week after that, she was so mad that she'd almost been made a widow, and us all orphans, for the sake of a silly apparition." Sheila shook her head; she could remember the fight as if it had been yesterday.

"Did he ever go back to try to find it?" Jenna asked.

"No, he was too embarrassed, what with Mom saying he was seeing things and threatening to leave him if he ever set foot on the beach again. You didn't argue with Mom – she wasn't very big, but she was very forceful. She kept Dad in his place! He couldn't manage her like he managed his horses!" Sheila smiled to herself. "Anyway, *I think* he was too frightened to go back – you know how superstitious he is. *I think* he thought he was being lured to his death by a ghost horse or some such nonsense!"

Jenna had wanted to ask more questions, but at that moment her mother had come into the kitchen and started talking to Sheila about work schedules and whether Sheila wanted to be in on the evening of the holiday. Riding along a quiet country lane, Jenna was going over the conversation again in her head when a pheasant in full summer plumage shot out of the hedge and flew right under Gold who leapt in alarm and kicked out at his supposed attacker. For a split second Jenna didn't know what was happening; there was a loud squawk as the bird rebounded from the kick and the sky and the ground seemed to be in the wrong places. Jenna very

nearly fell off, and it was by pure luck that she found herself
still in the saddle a few seconds later when Gold came back
down to earth, turning sharply and containing his urge to
run. On the pavement lay the pheasant, his glorious feathers
glinting in the sunlight as the life drained from him.

Steve jumped down and picked him up gently.

"Poor thing," he said, "Pheasants are a liability to themselves at this time of the year, strutting about, not looking
where they're going."

"I think Gold thought it was out to get him," said Jenna,
sad to see the lifeless body, but intrigued at the astonishing
colors of the bird's plumage.

Gold sniffed at the pheasant gingerly and snorted loudly.

"I was going to suggest that we hang it from your saddle
and take it home for your Mom to cook – but we might be
accused of poaching it if anyone sees us."

Steve laid the bird on the grass verge and mounted Giselle
and they rode on to Pendle Mount in silence again. It was
quite some time before Jenna's heart rate returned to normal.

✳ ✳ ✳ ✳ ✳

"I'll hold Gold while you go and ask about the horses," Steve
offered, jumping down from the saddle, wincing slightly as
the hard ground jarred an old back injury.

It had taken them a little under two hours to get to the café
on the bike path, and both horses and riders had enjoyed the
pace, which had been fast and furious, over the soft ground
of Pendle Mount.

"If it is all right to tie them up. Do you want to have a
drink here?" Jenna asked him, stretching her legs to rid her
ankles of a small ache.

"Only if you're buying. I don't have any money."

"You've never got any money," Jenna teased him, "Luckily I have. Dad always insists I keep some in my saddle bag in case of an emergency – though I have no idea what sort of emergency could be sorted out for the price of two sodas."

"My dad used to make me carry a piece of string when I was a kid – here…" Steve fished in his pocket and pulled out a roll of twine. "I still do, though I can honestly say I've never had to use it yet!"

It was hard to imagine Steve as a little boy, thought Jenna as she lined up for the drinks. She carried them out on a tray to where Steve was standing by a picnic bench with both horses' reins over his arm.

"The man said it was fine about the horses. He even said he'd bring them a bucket of water in a minute," Jenna told him as she swapped Gold's reins for one of the drinks.

She perched on the edge of the bench and gave Gold a sugar lump, and regretted it immediately because he kept nudging her for more and most of her drink spilled. Despite this, it seemed a very pleasant, civilized thing to be doing – sipping soda on a warm summer's morning in the company of Steve, Gold and Giselle.

"What's James up to today?" Steve asked her.

"Working at the bookshop," she answered, wondering if she'd tell James she'd been out with Steve when he phoned her later.

"Everything still good between you two?" Steve asked the question casually enough, so he wasn't prepared for the little barb of ice that shot through his heart when he heard her reply.

"Yes, really good, thanks. James is even thinking about taking a year off before going to college, and getting a job near here so we can see each other more often."

Jenna wasn't sure why she had said this. It wasn't true. But as the words left her mouth she studied Steve's face for a reaction, holding his gaze bravely. She was rewarded by the merest flicker of a cloud that passed unmistakably over his mesmerizing blue eyes.

Gold lifted his head sharply at the sound of hooves and sent the remains of Jenna's soda into her lap. He watched as three horses passed along the track. Two were ridden by novice, vacation riders, identifiable as such by their inappropriate footwear and lolling positions, and the third, much to Jenna's embarrassment, was Sarah. She was riding a tall, proud-looking gray gelding and the contrast with her companions was acute. A little bit like a swan who has found itself the foster parent of a pair of eager goslings, Steve thought to himself, as he watch the trio pass with mild interest.

"Hi, Sarah," Jenna called.

Sarah deliberately caught Jenna's eye as she rode past, but said nothing.

"How rude! Who does she think she is?" Steve exclaimed when the three had passed.

But Jenna just shrugged a reply; her insides churned with embarrassment, but she tried not to let the warmth and good feeling go out of her day.

chapter five

The first riding guests arrived late one Friday evening and Jenna was in the yard with her father, ready to greet them. The cream-colored horse trailer drove slowly through the gates and stopped at the end of the yard. A woman jumped down from the cab and came toward them smiling. She had a tanned, attractive face and warmly shook hands with Dave and Jenna.

"Hi, I'm Zoë, and this is Helen," she said, gesturing toward a second lady who was dark and small and pretty.

"Did you have a good trip?" Dave asked.

"Yes, the traffic wasn't too bad considering the time of year. I'd like to get the horses out, though; they'll want to stretch their legs."

Jenna watched with interest as a small, mahogany bay Arab was led down the ramp. He was both pretty and tough looking at the same time, and he inspected his surroundings with an air of confidence. The ramp shook as the second horse rushed down it, and Jenna smiled with pleasure at the bright bay mare who was looking around with such curiosity. She stood at about sixteen hands high, a well-muscled, stout mare with a broad white blaze and four white socks. Her eyes were very bright and very kind, and Jenna instinctively liked her and appreciated her quality.

"I've got two stables ready for them," she told Zoë and Helen, "or would you rather turn them straight out into the paddock after their trip?"

"The paddock, I think. It's what they're used to at home."

Jenna led the way, chatting comfortably with the two women and liking their obvious enjoyment of the historic stable yard and grounds of the Green Horse Hotel. She felt sure she was going to enjoy their company over the next few days and was looking forward to showing them the beautiful countryside and introducing Gold to them, too. She could hardly believe that her father was going to pay her to have so much fun – it beat cleaning bedrooms any day.

✳ ✳ ✳ ✳ ✳

Over the following few days Jenna and Gold rode for miles with Zoë and Helen. Each day they set off with maps and food and explored the local countryside. Once, when rain came down unexpectedly, they sheltered in some woods and Jenna phoned her father who drove out to meet them with their raincoats and a flask of hot coffee to revive them for their ride home. On another magical early morning, before the arrival of the beach parties, they galloped along the sands at the safe end of Rush Bay and paddled in the sea. Jenna scanned the water, looking for the Sand Horse, but the tide was high and there was nothing to see. She wondered if she should tell her new friends about the mysterious horse, but something stopped her.

By the end of the first week of having horsy guests at the hotel, Jenna was more exhausted than she had ever been in her life. It was harder even than the week she'd spent at Harry Houseman's stable, she told James on the phone one evening.

"I have to get up at six to do the morning feeds, then there are two extra stalls to muck out and *then* I have to be ready by nine and looking half-way awake and tidy to ride out with them for the day."

"It sounds more fun than working in the bookshop," James sighed. He was missing Jenna much more than she was missing him, by the sound of it. "The most exciting thing that happened to me today was a woman complaining that there were too many long words in a book that she'd bought. As if I could do anything about that!"

"Are you riding Charlie much?" Jenna asked.

"Not really. Alice is away, staying with her friend, and it isn't as much fun by yourself," James was definitely feeling sorry for himself. Jenna could hear that from the tone of his voice. "It's a long time until I'm going to see you again. August is still weeks away."

"Only three weeks, and then you'll be here for a month. We'll probably be sick of the sight of each other after all that time," Jenna was getting tired of having to cheer James up, and there was an edge to her voice.

"Don't get mad, Jen. I only want to see you. It's not much to ask!"

"Well, why don't I ask Mom and Dad if you can come and stay this weekend? Then you can help with the horses… the mucking out in particular!"

"Do you think your parents would let me? I don't think they'd mind at the bookshop if I took a couple of days off. I often don't have that much to do, and I think they only gave me the job because the owner is a friend of Dad's," James said. His spirits began to rise with the prospect of being with Jenna.

"I'll ask Mom and Dad now. I don't suppose they'll mind – I'll call you back later when I've talked to them!" And without saying goodbye, Jenna switched off the phone and rushed from the room.

"Bye, Jenna… I… I love you…" James whispered down the empty airways, brave for once because he knew she couldn't hear him.

* * * * *

Dave and Angie were happy for James to come and stay, Angie in particular approved of his friendship with Jenna if only because it took her daughter's mind off Steve. Jenna was delighted for at least two reasons. First, she was genuinely excited that James was coming, and that pleased her as she had been finding it difficult to maintain much enthusiasm for a long-distance relationship that amounted to gloomy phone calls and infrequent weekend dates. Secondly, she was looking forward to having some help. Despite her preference for cleaning up after horses over cleaning up after guests, she was finding the work extremely tiring.

James was to have the spare room in the hotel's private living quarters, as he was a guest of the family rather than the paying variety. He arrived on Friday evening in the cute little car that he shared with his mother.

"She said I could have it for the weekend. Secretly I think she's glad to get rid of me for a while. She's fed up with me moping around the house every night," James told Jenna.

He swung her around in a great big, overwhelming bear hug that left her breathless.

"You idiot!" Jenna gasped, but she was very glad to see him.

"The Dixons phoned this afternoon, Jen. They're arriving just before lunch tomorrow and want the stables ready for them," Dave told his daughter over a rare family meal in honor of James' stay.

They were eating early in the dining room, before the restaurant was open to the guests, as a special treat.

"My charges for next week," Jenna explained to James. "I hope they're nice; Zoë and Helen were lovely, and they really seemed to enjoy themselves."

43

"Mrs. Dixon sounded a bit fussy," Dave told her, "She asked lots of questions about the quality of the hay we're providing and wanted to know if you're qualified to look after her horses."

"What did you tell her?" Angie asked.

"I said you had a GHHHC," Dave told them, wiping gravy from his beard with a white linen napkin. "That seemed to satisfy her."

"What on earth is that?" Jenna laughed, "and why don't I remember getting it?"

"Oh, haven't you had it yet? I must have forgotten to sign it and mail it to you! You are probably unique, the only person so far to be awarded the Green Horse Hotel Horse Masters Certificate. I'd better award James one while I'm at it. We can't have the guests complaining about unqualified staff!"

James and Jenna got up early and worked very hard the next morning. By eleven o'clock the stables were clean, the yard was swept and there was fresh straw and racks full of soft, sweet hay in the two stalls prepared especially for the Dixons' horses.

"There, that ought to satisfy the fussiest of owners," James said, leaning his broom against a wall with the other stable tools. "What do you think, Steve?"

Steve had just returned from a trip to the feed store. He hadn't really needed to go, but was tactfully keeping out of the way of the young couple.

"I'm impressed; I haven't seen it look this good for ages. Who are you expecting, royalty?"

"I hope not. Just another two guests bringing their horses, but Dad thinks they might be the fussy types."

"Well there's nothing they could find fault with here, Jen," Steve told her.

"It was James, mostly. He's been wonderful. He hosed down the stalls and swept the yard and did all the heavy work," Jenna smiled her thanks to James.

Steve went off to retrieve his saddle, unreasonably glad that the wonderful James was only around for the weekend.

Jenna realized that Steve had been very wrong when Mrs. Dixon arrived, as she immediately found fault with a great number of things. She was a tall, handsome, blonde woman, wearing lots of make-up. First it was the gateway, which was too narrow for her to drive her trailer through, even though Dave Wells pointed out that trailers much wider than Mrs. Dixon's vehicle comfortably managed it. Then the beautiful old stables came in for criticism. They were too dark, too draughty, the cobbles might harbor germs and the feeders couldn't have been cleaned properly. She looked Jenna up and down critically, trying to determine her age. It was obvious to Mrs. Dixon that Jenna was just a teenager, however well qualified her father said she was.

It was clear from the start that Jenna was expected to act as groom and do everything for the horses.

Mrs. Dixon stood back and gave instructions. "Get the horses out, please. They've been traveling a long way," she said impatiently.

James and Jenna let down the ramp and, taking one horse each, led them to the stables. Jenna found herself with a kindly chestnut mare, a Thoroughbred of about sixteen hands. James was in charge of a gray gelding, a middleweight, slightly taller than the mare. They were nice horses, beautifully turned out and very well mannered – unlike their owner, Jenna thought to herself with a smile.

"Sugar and Spice!" Jenna read the names on the little brass tags that were attached to the soft leather head collars. She ran her hands over Sugar's smooth chestnut neck. "They're beautifully groomed. I wonder if Mrs. Dixon does them herself."

James snorted his skepticism.

"I doubt it. She didn't even want to take them off the trailer herself. These two are obviously boarded somewhere. Mrs. Dixon is used to paying to have everything done for her; you can tell by the way she gives orders instead of asking politely. I hate people who do that."

Dave Wells appeared in the doorway.

"It's all right, you can come out. She's gone…" he said in an exaggerated stage whisper.

"Gone? Where?"

"I unhitched the trailer for her and she sped off to the station to collect her husband – apparently he didn't want to travel down with the horses," Dave told them.

"Couldn't bear to be in the car with her for four hours, more likely," said James.

"Well, you'd think with all that fuss she made about the stables she'd want to see that her precious horses were safely installed, and not just leave them with strangers and drive off." Jenna would never have done that to Gold.

"It takes all sorts, Jen. I've learned that much from being in the hotel trade. Just bite your tongue, do everything reasonable that she asks, and tell yourself she won't be here forever! That's what I always do."

Mr. and Mrs. Dixon quickly made themselves known to the staff of the hotel, and not for being nice and kind and polite. First they were rude to Sheila, accusing her of bringing the wrong wine, and then they upset Angie, saying her desserts, (for which she was fast becoming famous), were boring and too full of cream. They even managed to annoy Steve when, thinking he was on the payroll, they ordered him to clean their tack for them.

46

Jenna wasn't looking forward to the first day's riding with them. It wasn't as bad as she'd expected, though it wasn't a great deal of fun either. The Dixons' idea of Jenna's role in the procedures was to be there to act as a guide only when specifically asked and to keep quiet at all other times. Gold was confused. He was used to striding out alongside companion horses, not being kept back out of the way. Jenna was slightly relieved. She hadn't known how she was going to make conversation with these strange, unfriendly people and was glad not to have to bother. She wished James was with her, but apart from Steve's horses, which were in training, there was only old Tufty at home and his riding days were over.

It was quite difficult keeping Gold behind as he had a naturally long stride and an enthusiasm for haste at whatever pace he was going. Jenna suggested she should ride in front.

"Sugar likes to lead," was the curt reply she got from Mr. Dixon.

From behind, she was able to watch the Dixons, and she decided that for all their talk neither of them were good or confident riders. *They don't even seem to be enjoying themselves very much*, thought Jenna, *I wonder why they do it*? The day was perfect for riding, the sun was high, there was a light and gentle breeze lifting the leaves, and suddenly Jenna didn't care who she was with as long as she had Gold to ride and James waiting for her when she got home. It was his last day with them, but soon he would be back for a much longer visit and Jenna was looking forward to that very much. When they were apart it was easy to forget how much she liked him, how good-looking he was and how relaxed she felt in his company. Maybe he didn't have the charisma of Steve or his dangerous air of mystery, but he was kind and honest, and though she'd never heard him say it, Jenna knew that James loved her.

"Turn left at the crossroads, and take the trail," she called to Mrs. Dixon, coming out of her daydream. "Then you can canter all the way to the top of that hill. The ground is good enough and there is an amazing view across to the coast."

Gold jumped and fussed and was threatening to rear when Jenna told him that he must let the other horses go in front. She held him back until she was sure he couldn't catch up before letting him go. The surge of power was astonishing. *This is what it must feel like to be shot from a cannon*, Jenna thought to herself, and she fought to regain control as they galloped up the hill. The Dixons were waiting for her at the top, and she could feel their eyes on her as she raced toward them. She knew how good she looked on a horse and she knew that her horse was special. She rode him with pride and a wide grin, halting him expertly and even allowing him to do his little half rear because she knew it looked impressive. – He was showing off, and for once she didn't care and showed off with him.

At the café, Jenna was expected to hold all the horses because Mr. Dixon insisted that Spice didn't like to be tied up. Jenna didn't mind. The horses were far better company than their owners, though she would have liked a drink. Jenna noticed that both the Dixons were walking a little stiffly when they returned from their coffee break, which had lasted almost an hour. *They're not as fit as they thought they were*, she thought to herself smiling.

"There are two ways home from here," she told them. "One takes about an hour, and the other about two hours."

She wasn't surprised when they chose the quick way home, and she hummed to herself as she rode, looking forward to a cool drink and a plate of Angie's special ham and cheese sandwiches.

chapter six

When they got back to the stables, the Dixons just handed Jenna their reins and hobbled away, heading for the hotel.

Gold was impatient and got too close to Spice who spun around, threatening to kick, and Jenna got in a tangle with the reins. Luckily Steve was in Giselle's stall combing the mare's mane, and he came to Jenna's rescue and took Gold, silently despairing at the mentality of people who cared so little about their horses that they wouldn't even untack them themselves. He helped Jenna until James came hurrying down to the yard, and then he slipped back into Giselle's stall, preferring the mare's company to James's.

Still in her jodhpurs, but having discarded her boots and socks, Jenna wriggled her hot toes luxuriously in the thick cool clover on the lawn behind the house. She felt sleepy and relaxed as she sat in the garden chair and sipped from a glass of ice water.

"We've got the rest of the day to ourselves," said Jenna, "thanks to the Dixons' lack of stamina. And you're not driving home until this evening, so what do you want to do?"

James thought about this. In truth he didn't mind what he did as long as he was with Jenna.

"Are there any jobs your dad would like us to do?" he asked. He was the sort who liked to repay hospitality if he could.

"I bet there are plenty, but I'm not asking him! I was thinking more along the lines of going to the beach."

"It will be very crowded. I've never really seen the point in sitting on a beach with a load of other people, but if you want to…"

They sat in silence for a while longer, both deep in thought.

"We could bathe the horses. That's always a nice job on a hot day. I'll even comb the tangles out of Tufty's mane for you," James suggested.

"All right, let's do that," said Jenna, shutting her eyes and enjoying the warm sun on her face, "but let's just sit here for a bit longer!"

The bathing soon turned into a water fight. It was an accident, James insisted, when he dropped the hose and it squirted all over Jenna. The bucket of water she threw over him in reply was far from accidental and her aim was good. Gasping and spluttering, James picked up the hose, and before long neither of them had a dry stitch of clothing.

Gold was interested. He liked water, and watched, ears pricked, as they cavorted around the yard screaming and yelling and laughing.

Tufty was not impressed or much surprised these days by the human species. He liked it when they fed him and he liked it when they talked to him softly and stroked or scratched his neck. It was when they got silly, like now, that he despaired of them and he blocked his mind to their unseemly behavior and tried to go to sleep.

Tufty wasn't the only one having curmudgeonly feelings. In the tack room, which doubled as an office, Steve was trying to make his accounts balance for the month, a task insisted upon by his father who had put money into the training venture. It was the only thing to do with preparing racehorses that Steve wasn't very good at and the one he least enjoyed. The sound of Jenna having fun with James was almost too much to bear when he was stuck inside on such a beautiful day. He turned up his radio and drowned out the noises of other people having a good time.

✳ ✳ ✳ ✳ ✳

Jenna got her orders from her father the next morning when they sat and had breakfast together. Dave Wells cut the top off his boiled egg and sprinkled it with salt as he told her what the Dixons wanted her to do.

"They were in the restaurant late last night, moaning about how stiff they were from riding, when they hit upon the idea of getting you to do the riding for them. They're going to drive to the beach and they want you to take their horses and meet them there so that they can ride along the sands. It's a lifetime's ambition for Mrs. Dixon. Apparently she does have a soft romantic side, and it's more or less the whole reason they're here."

"Do they want me to ride one and lead the other all the way to Rush Bay?" Jenna asked, wondering what Honey was like to ride.

"Yes, you've done that sort of thing before."

"Why can't they take them in the trailer?"

"Because they have a lunch appointment with some friends and won't have time to bring the horses back again, and because they are lazy to the bone, though don't quote me on that, and because they like it when other people do things for them. I suspect it makes them feel important. Is it safe for you to do it?" Dave looked at his daughter searchingly. He was undoubtedly a businessman, but he was an adoring

51

father first and foremost and Jenna meant more to him than she would ever have believed. He was getting heartily sick of the Dixons making unreasonable demands and upsetting his staff and his family.

"I think so. The roads are mostly quiet and their horses are very well behaved, and I certainly won't miss the Dixons' company!" Jenna answered.

"So you'll do it?"

"Yes. It'll give me the chance to have another look for Mr. Penrose's Sand Horse while they're riding."

"Thanks, honey, I'll give you a bonus after all this. You'll be careful not to go near the quicksand, won't you?"

* * * * *

Jenna decided that she was missing James when she was mucking out the stables after breakfast. He had left the evening before. They'd spent ages saying goodbye; the moon was very high before James finally got into his car and drove away. Jenna finished the mucking out and took Tufty's feed down to his paddock. She stroked his smooth, clean, tangle-free mane and thought about James and how much she liked him when they were together. The trouble was, she quickly forgot him when he wasn't there and went back to thinking about Steve again. Jenna was aware of how strong James's feelings for her were, and doubted she was being fair to him. It was all so difficult and confusing when you liked two people very much.

She put tack on Sugar and Spice; both horses wore expensive, beautifully kept saddles and bridles. She clipped a leather lead rein to Spice's snaffle bit rings and mounted from the block in the yard.

Steve came out to see her off and held the gate open with a mock bow as she swept through it with her hands full.

52

"It's a fantastic day for a ride. The Dixons don't know what they're missing," Steve told her, thinking how pretty she looked.

"They do, though, aching legs and sore rear ends! They could hardly walk when they got off yesterday. Mrs. Dixon looked like a chicken."

Steve laughed out loud. He loved it when Jenna made him laugh, and she loved to do it. It made her feel clever and special.

"Are you missing James yet?" It seemed he was unable to stop himself asking.

"Yes, a bit, especially when I had to do all the mucking out by myself."

"I'd be really hurt if I was James and I thought you only wanted me for my skills with a shovel," Steve told her, holding her gaze in the hope of learning more.

Jenna just smiled at him and gave him a look which could have meant anything, (but obviously meant something), as she rode off on the gentle chestnut mare with the tall gelding jogging peacefully at her side.

* * * * *

"We've been here forever," Mr. Dixon said crossly as Jenna arrived at the parking lot three minutes after the appointed time.

Jenna knew this wasn't true because she'd seen their car pull up as she'd ridden over the headland toward Rush Bay. It took some effort, but she just smiled at him and, ignoring his remark, said, "It's a lovely day for a gallop along the beach."

She helped Mrs. Dixon mount Sugar and held the stirrup on the offside for Mr. Dixon while he hauled himself into Spice's saddle. She watched as they rode away and wondered why they seemed so cross all the time. It must be exhausting, she thought to herself. Judging that she had about an hour before they returned, Jenna walked quickly along the cliff path away from the beach, and headed for the place where she had first seen the Sand Horse. The tide was out a long way, as far as Jenna had ever seen it. She scanned the beach for the Dixons, and smiled when she saw them, because they looked like two dolls on tiny toy horses cantering away across the sand.

The view from the cliff path was breathtaking and Jenna, puffing slightly from the warm climb, stopped to stare at the horizon as it blended almost imperceptibly from blue sea to blue sky. She walked on, not wanting to look for the horse until she was in exactly the same spot as she had been before, a little afraid that the magic, should magic be needed, would only work if everything was as it had been before. She knew the place; it was where a clump of sea pinks grew near a huge granite outcrop. Suddenly it seemed very important to her that she should see the Sand Horse again, if only for Mr. Penrose's sake, so that his daughter would believe him. Jenna stood at the edge of the cliff, her eyes drawn down to her feet, and it felt as if she were afraid of something, afraid that the Sand Horse wouldn't be there. A feather caught her eye and she bent to pick it up. It was big, with a blunt tip. Broad chocolate and cream-colored bars divided its length, and Jenna knew, because Steve had once found one for her, that it was a buzzard's feather. Finding strength from this residue of nature, she looked down to the sands below, scanning with her eyes along the tide line and the shallow water beyond it.

At first she saw nothing, and disappointment flooded through her. There was nothing there, just lines and lines of rippled sand, dotted with stones. Then she spotted a familiar shape, further up the beach than she remembered. It was almost covered, just a vague, shadowy form in the sand, just as if some clever person had fashioned a horse's head with spade and smoothing hand, then let the tide wash over it and slowly take it away.

Jenna was running before she knew why, scrambling down the cliff path, slipping and sliding with no fear or sense of danger. She could see that the tide was turning and she had to know what was there before it was covered over again. She reached the rocks and jumped with a dull thud on to the deep dry sand and kept on running, keeping her eyes on the exact spot she had located from above, though there was nothing to be seen now. As she ran toward it, all seemed flat, no stones, no seaweed, no gulls walking along the tide's edge. She was almost upon it before she saw the horse clearly, though it seemed, like a vision, to be disappearing before her very eyes. It was a carved wooden statue, worn and damaged by the sea but still proud and angry, with a mouth baring teeth and a wild, wicked look in its weathered eye. Jenna had only a few seconds to take it all in, because suddenly, terrifyingly, her feet started sinking. Her ankles had disappeared and she stared stupidly at the rising sand for a moment. Realization came to her with a sickening jolt as she remembered the sinking sands and threw herself backwards onto the ground. Had anyone been watching from the cliff they might have thought she had stepped on some explosives, so violent were her efforts to stop herself sinking. Jenna rolled and rolled, coughing and spluttering as sand and salt water got in her mouth and nose but not caring, so thankful was she to feel the soft sand becoming firm enough to take her weight again. When she finally stopped turning she lay there for some time, unable to believe what she had done, unable to understand what had come over her. What had possessed her to behave so foolishly? She rose to her feet and walked slowly back up the beach, past the large sign warning her not to go on. She was covered in sand that stuck to her wet clothes and the buzzard's feather, sadly bedraggled, was still gripped tightly in her hand.

The sun started to dry the sand, which began to stick crisply to Jenna's face and hair. She was embarrassed when a woman walking her dog stared at her and asked if she was all right.

"Yes, thanks, I just tripped. I'll be dry soon," she said smiling, trying to appear normal, though her heart was pounding in her chest as she thought about the narrow escape she'd had. Why had she done it? She knew the sands were treacherous. Her dad had warned her only the night before, and yet she had just started running, mindful of nothing but seeing the Sand Horse. There was something else too, something disturbing her thoughts, like a memory she couldn't quite grasp. It was almost as if it had happened to her before, but she was quite sure it hadn't.

Jenna was grateful to sit down on a bench in the parking lot, and even more grateful that she'd arrived back before the Dixons, whom she saw walking their horses up the beach path toward her. She brushed at her clothes in an attempt to clean herself up; she'd been shocked when she caught sight of her reflection in a car window. She looked strange, still in her riding hat, covered in damp sand and with a graze on her left cheek.

For the first time since she'd met them the Dixons were in good spirits. The gallop on the beach had been a success and both had color in their pallid, city cheeks and unaccustomed smiles on their normally irritated lips. They didn't seem to notice Jenna's bedraggled state as they handed her their reins, but they did stop to pat their horses and say nice things to them, before Mrs. Dixon tottered stiffly back to their car.

"Just walk them home, Jenna," Mr. Dixon instructed, "They've had quite a gallop this morning."

"Yes of course I will, they've worked hard for you," Jenna said politely, "Shall I ride Spice and lead Sugar this time?"

Mr. Dixon stared at Jenna blankly.

"I don't think you understand, young lady. I meant *you* walk them home. They've both had a long gallop; I don't want you to ride *either* of them back. Understand?" The sunshine that had touched him for a few magical minutes now left his face again and he was the same stressed, middle-aged man who was his own boss and used to having his own way, however unreasonable. "Anyway, you're not in a fit state to ride. Look, your clothes are all covered in sand. It would scratch the saddles."

Jenna didn't trust herself to say anything, but there were plenty of things she'd have liked to shout at his narrow shoulders as he turned and walked away from her. She thought about her father and the words stayed in her head. How did *he* manage to keep so calm when dealing with people like that? Jenna wished she knew.

She watched, open mouthed, as the Dixons' car started up and drove away. She was wet, she'd nearly fallen into quicksand, she was tired, she was hot, her riding boots felt tight and now she had *miles* to walk home. Jenna had had enough of taking guests riding… she'd rather clean bathrooms any day!

✳ ✳ ✳ ✳ ✳

An hour later the sun was really high, and it beat down on Jenna's bare head as she was carrying her riding hat, unable to suffer its restrictions any longer. She had blisters on both heels and she was feeling sick and a little giddy and had to hold on to Spice's stirrup for support. Both horses were behaving very well, but their strides were longer than Jenna's and she had to jog to keep step with them. The heat was unbearable. She took off her tee shirt, thankful that she was wearing a sports bra underneath which was substantial enough to pass as an athletic top. All she could think of was getting as far as the quarry lake, and the promise of the cold water drove her on. When they finally got there, to the surprise of a silent fisherman, Jenna strode in up to her knees, not caring that the water rushed into her leather boots as she splashed her face over and over again with the cooling, energizing, silvery liquid. Sugar and Spice both drank greedily and noisily and water spurted back out over their bit rings. Jenna would have loved to drink too, but she wasn't quite desperate enough to trust the murky, fishy water. Feeling much better, she set off again to walk the last hour home, but it wasn't long before her sodden boots rubbed new blisters and walking became crippling.

"That's it," she said out loud, "I don't care what the Dixons say, I'm riding home."

Wearily she pulled herself on to Spice and adjusted his stirrups, which were far too long for her. Feeling achy and slightly dazed, she rode quietly back to the stables.

chapter seven

By the time Jenna reached the stables she was feeling
dreadfully sick. It was all she could do to stay upright as she
untacked the horses and gave them each a feed. Steve found
her a few minutes later retching into the tack room sink.

"Sweetheart, what's the matter? You look dreadful. Come
here," he put his arm around her shoulder and held her firmly
until the spasms of nausea had left her. Then he guided her
up to the house and delivered her to Angie who was having
a rare five minutes to herself in the garden.

"She's been sick and she's very hot. I expect she's had too
much sun. She says she hasn't fallen off or anything," Steve
told her because Jenna was sobbing in her mother's arms,
too wretched to speak.

"Thanks, Steve, I'll look after her now," Angie fussed
anxiously over her daughter.

"I'll see to the horses until you're feeling better, Jen,"
Steve told her, "It's rotten having sunstroke, but at least it
doesn't usually last too long."

He went back to the stables and picked up the saddles and
bridles which Jenna had left in a heap on the ground. Then
he gave the horses fresh water and filled up their hayracks.

When he heard voices in the yard he went out to see who it
was.

"Where's the girl?" Mrs. Dixon snapped.

Steve had found himself getting angry at the mere sight of

this arrogant woman and the sound of her voice did nothing to soothe him.

"She has a name, she's called Jenna. She's not feeling very well at the moment, so I am looking after the horses for her." His tone was slow and measured, his gaze steady.

Mrs. Dixon looked at him properly for the first time and found she was looking into the eyes of one of the most handsome men she had ever seen. She softened slightly and wondered why he seemed so protective of the girl, unless it was his kid sister, of course. She tried a different line of questioning.

"Do you work here?"

"No, I use the yard to train my racehorses. Jenna helps me sometimes," Steve replied, wondering why he was bothering to talk to this woman, who was so obviously not worth the effort.

"Oh, she *works* for you, does she?" Mrs. Dixon felt she understood: handsome, rich (he *had* to be if he owned race-horses) and one of the bosses; in other words he was the *same as she was*. In that case, she could do Steve a big favor, and who knew where that could lead?

"Then you'll be *very* interested to know that she can't be trusted. My husband told her quite clearly not to ride our horses home, but to lead them, and yet we saw her riding into the yard when we got back from lunch with our friends."

Steve could hardly believe his ears and for a few seconds he just opened his mouth but couldn't speak. Mrs. Dixon was gratified. It looked as though Jenna wouldn't be working with this young man's horses for much longer and she smiled to herself.

"You expected her to walk all the way back from Rush Bay?" Steve found his voice at last. "In this heat? Are you stupid, woman? Whatever were you thinking of?" Steve walked away to stop himself strangling her and thought how fortunate it was that it was Mrs. and not Mr. Dixon who was standing in front of him, because he wasn't sure he'd have been so restrained with a man.

"How dare you talk to me like that?" Mrs. Dixon had gotten over her shock and was spoiling for a fight. "We are being charged well over the going rate for her to look after our horses, and if she's not up to the job then the Hotel won't get a penny from us." She was furious, and a small bubble of spit had gathered at the corner of her mouth. She had become ugly with her anger, no longer the cool, composed handsome woman she thought herself to be. The sight of her made Steve laugh nastily. You couldn't argue with people who thought that money bought everything, but her cruelty to Jenna made him want to be cruel to her in return.

"Did you know that you are drooling?" he asked her. "It's very unattractive, but perhaps you can't help it at your age."

Steve hadn't said anything so petty and spiteful since he'd been at school and his words both shocked and delighted him in equal measure. It was funny what his feelings for Jenna made him do sometimes, he thought to himself as he brushed past a speechless Mrs. Dixon and went, whistling, on his way.

When Jenna woke the next morning she was greatly relieved to feel well again. The room had stopped spinning, and though her stomach still rumbled it was with the pleasant anticipation of breakfast. She sat up in bed, stretched, and looked around her room, wondering what she could do to make it seem more homely. The colors were warm and bright and she liked the patterned blinds, but apart from a few books and the posh teddy bear that James had given her, the shelves and the window sill were empty of interest as she had chosen to junk all her toys and childish ornaments in a big clean-up before the decorating had started. She regretted it now, just a bit, but she really was too old for sparkly knick-knacks and trinket boxes. Perhaps she would ask her Mom if there was anything around the hotel she could have to make her room look less bare. Looking at her watch, she was shocked to see that it was after ten o'clock. Had she really been asleep since yesterday? What would the Dixons say about their horses not being mucked out or groomed, or ready for them to ride? She dressed quickly and dashed out of her room, almost colliding with Angie who was carrying a tray of breakfast.

"Careful!" she said, smiling at Jenna, "I take it that you're feeling better."

"I was until I realized the time. The Dixons are going to be furious if their horses aren't ready."

"Ah, yes, well, the Dixons are not our problem any more," Angie told her, putting the tray down on Jenna's bedside table. "They've gone. They went yesterday evening while you were asleep."

"Why?"

"They gave lots of reasons in the end. They didn't like it that you rode Spice when they'd told you not to. They didn't like Steve being rude to them. They didn't like my cooking much either… but most of all they didn't like Dad telling them that they were the rudest people he had ever had the misfortune to have in his hotel!" Angie couldn't help herself from giggling at the memory of Mrs. Dixon's gaping mouth as she'd listened to Dave, who had finally lost control of his temper in front of a guest.

"Dad said that?" Jenna could hardly believe her ears. "After all he's ever said about biting his lip and letting it all wash over him!"

"It was the state you were in that finally made him flip. How can anyone be so selfish as to expect you to walk all that way? I'd like to see the Dixons do it!"

"What did Steve say that was so rude?" Jenna was intrigued. Steve was generally quite mild mannered and polite to people, even people he didn't much like.

"He wouldn't tell me, but he did apologize in case it reflected badly on the hotel."

"Is Dad very upset?"

"Not really, not about what happened. He's annoyed about them not paying their bill, though I don't suppose he'll do anything about it in case they complain to the Tourist Board. I think he's just relieved they've gone – we all are, for that matter." Angie poured milk onto Jenna's cereal and passed it to her. "You may as well eat this here, seeing as I took the trouble to bring you breakfast in bed.

Jenna sat back down on her bed and began to eat.

"Mom?"

"Yes, darling?"

"Can I look around the hotel and choose one or two knick-knacks for my room?"

"Of course. I was wondering if you'd regret getting rid of so much stuff before we redecorated."

"I do a bit, I suppose, but I didn't want it to look like a little girl's room anymore."

"Well, why not take some things from the room you were in, though not that gloomy picture, of course. I'm sure that was what was giving you nightmares."

"Thanks, there's a blue vase in there that I liked, and a glass bowl. I'll get them later."

There was something else on Jenna's mind.

"Mom?"

"Yes, hon?"

"Mom, I saw the Sand Horse again yesterday, clearly this time. It looks like a wooden carving."

"Really? Like a rocking horse?" Angie had always had a liking for rocking horses, having had one as child.

"Bigger than that, I think, though I could only see its head."

"I wonder why it doesn't float away," Angie said, "Are you sure it wasn't just an odd-shaped rock?"

"It looked like wood. I think I can remember seeing the grain. It was pretty beat up, though."

"Maybe when the season is over we can all go down and look for it," Angie suggested, wishing she had more time to spend with her daughter.

"I'd like that." Jenna felt as though she needed her mom and dad with her the next time she dared to go near the sands. "I thought I'd go and see Mr. Penrose about it later and tell him what I saw."

"That's a good idea. Sheila was saying this morning that she's a bit worried about him, says he's been getting very tired lately; though at eighty-seven, what can you expect?"

They chatted for a while longer, enjoying each other's company until both remembered things they had to do and felt compelled to go and do them.

* * * * *

When Jenna eventually got down to the stables she found them deserted. Steve was riding Giselle, Gold was turned out in the paddock with Tufty, and the two stalls that had been the temporary homes of Sugar and Spice stood empty and clean. The mucking out had been done, and Jenna, feeling gratefully unneeded, decided to go and check out the knick-knacks she'd asked her mom about.

She wandered back through the hotel and went to the reception desk to collect the key and make sure that there was no one booked into room three, which was where Jenna had slept when her own room was being decorated. Room three was at the end of a corridor that caught the afternoon sun through old leaded glass windows overlooking the kitchen gardens. Jenna let herself in and looked around. The first thing that caught her eye was the painting of the huge seas and the floundering ship, and it sent a strange feeling through her body as she was immediately reminded of her own recent, watery fright. She didn't want to look at the painting so she stood with her back to it and studied the knick-knacks on the windowsill instead. There was an eclectic mix of *object d'art* and Jenna chose a blue vase, a crystal bowl, a ship in a bottle and an oddly-shaped decanter which had a dusty string of colored glass beads wrapped loosely around its neck. She gave a lot of consideration to this last piece. It was old and rather dull as the once clear glass was now frosted and cloudy, but there was something about the shape, heavy at the bottom with a slim, elegant neck that attracted her. At least, she thought that was what attracted her; certainly something seemed to be telling her that it would look just right in her newly decorated room. The beads were pretty. Jenna turned the decanter over in her hands and held it up to the light. As she did so, she noticed for the first time a small inscription engraved on the surface of the roughened glass. She stared hard and read 'The Pegasus'. *What has an old decanter got to do with a winged horse?* she wondered as she inspected the beads. They were threaded on a dry leather thong that threatened to crack with age as she unwound it. Jenna slipped them around her wrist and studied them on her bare, brown arm. She didn't like the feeling of intense cold or the weight of them, which seemed to press into her skin, so she took them off quickly and replaced them on the decanter.

Jenna left room three with her arms full and took her treasures to her own bedroom where she spent several minutes trying things out in different places. She put the jug and the bottle on her dresser, and the bowl looked lovely on the windowsill; sunlight streamed through it and spilled its blue glow across the painted surface. The decanter was more problematic. Wherever she tried it, it just looked shabby, which indeed it was.

"I'll take it back," she said to herself, "later, after I've ridden Gold."

She left the decanter on her bed and went out into the sunshine. When Angie came into Jenna's room later, with a basket full of clean wash, she picked up the decanter and was puzzled by Jenna's choice.

"It is a nice color, and the beads are very pretty. I'll put some dried flowers in it later," she mused. She placed it on the windowsill and went on with her work.

Jenna rode Gold fast despite the hot day. It seemed like a treat to be by herself for a change, and not the nursemaid to less experienced riders, however nice (or not) they were. She was expecting more guests, but not until the weekend, and in the meantime she looked forward to jumping Gold in the paddock at home, with Steve's critical eye upon her. She trotted back through the village and stopped by Mr. Penrose's cottage, scanning the tidy garden and squinting at the windows for signs that the old man was at home. Jenna saw no one save a ginger cat stalking through the vegetable patch, hiding behind a line of lettuce plants with his eye firmly fixed on a careless robin, which was busy with a snail. The cat was large and clumsy with heavy trousers of fluff, and he looked too fat for hunting, Jenna thought. As if to prove her right, the cat took aim too early and the robin flew away.

Jenna called to Mr. Penrose, but when he didn't answer she decided to come back later.

"Take these with you, if you're going to see Mr. Penrose," Dave handed his daughter two paperback books, "I said he could have them. He wanted something good to read because he's spending less time in the garden. Poor old chap, he looked worn out when I saw him last."

"All right," said Jenna, as she sat on the back doorstep and tied the laces of her sneakers.

"Oh, and Jenna, Mom asked me to ask you if you could help in the restaurant tomorrow night, seeing as you haven't got any extra horses here until Friday."

Jenna was tempted to ask if she'd get paid extra for the waitressing, but then she remembered that the Dixons had left without paying their bill and thought better of it.

"Yes, of course," she said sweetly, smiling at her father, who was chomping on a large chocolate bar, safe in the knowledge that his wife was at the supermarket.

Jenna ran down to the village, her long legs carrying her swiftly along the paved road, past the church and the village shop and on to the row of cottages where Mr. Penrose lived. She went up the garden path, pausing to stroke the ginger cat that was now stretched out sleepily under a small camellia bush. The cat offered his tummy to be tickled, but when Jenna obliged he grabbed her arm with all four feet and bit and scratched and kicked her ferociously. Yelling and pulling her arm away at the same time, Jenna was shocked to see a trickle of blood run down her wrist. She cursed under her breath and the cat stared at her with his large, round, green eyes flashing.

"Don't take it out on me," Jenna told the cat, "just because you're fat and useless at catching birds, it's not *my* fault."

Jenna knocked at the door and stood there a while, inspecting the damage done to her arm. When no one answered she peeped quickly through the window into the dark sitting room where Mr. Penrose usually sat reading his paper. The armchair was empty, so Jenna walked around to the back and tried to look in through the kitchen window, but the curtains were still drawn. It was worrisome. Mr. Penrose was always at home, unless he had walked up to the village shop to get his paper. Jenna left the books on the step and sprinted back through the village. She stuck her head around the door of the shop. There were no customers and Mrs. Berry, who ran the shop, was sitting on a very low stool behind the counter with a coin in her hands and a small pile of scratch cards.

"Have you seen Mr. Penrose today?" Jenna asked.

"No dear, he hasn't been in for his paper yet. Would you like to take it for him?" She stood up with some difficulty, and Jenna was sure she could hear her knees creaking.

"It's just that he doesn't seem to be answering at home. I suppose he could be out, but it's odd that he hasn't collected his paper yet," Jenna told her, wondering why she felt so panicky.

Mrs. Berry looked at her watch, "Well, I've never known him be this late before," she said. "Perhaps you'd better go over to his daughter's. You might find him there."

Sheila Penrose lived at the other end of the village in a small housing development. Jenna wasn't sure of the number, but she ran down there and asked a small boy on a bicycle, who told her which one it was. For the second time that day Jenna was out of luck. She banged on the front door several times, but only succeeded in annoying Sheila's dog, who was shut in the house and barking to be let out.

"Well, they could be out together," she thought to herself, but she still felt uneasy as she jogged back to Mr. Penrose's cottage to collect the books.

She tried one last time, knocking hard on the newly painted door, but no one came. As she passed the sitting room window, she peered through it again at the empty armchair in the corner of the room. With a start she noticed the tartan throw that Mr. Penrose used to wrap around his legs, dropped untidily on the floor; then a dreadful, sickening feeling came over her as she made out the shape of a slippered foot lying in the doorway to the kitchen.

Later, whenever Jenna allowed herself to think about it, she wondered how she had found the courage to open the door and step into the little, dark cottage. She knew that if she *had* stopped to think about what she might find there, she never could have done it. But she didn't stop. She only wanted to help Mr. Penrose back to his feet, to lead him to his armchair and to make him a cup of strong, sweet tea, which would surely make him feel better. She had entered the house, through the door, which she knew was rarely locked, and into the room where the old man was lying. Jenna knelt down beside him and stared at his lifeless form. His chest was sunken and ominously still and she knew instinctively that there was no need to feel for a pulse. His skin was papery and pale and his eyes were shut. His clothes seemed too huge for his wasted frame, as if he had somehow faded away as he had lain there. Jenna noticed his white, bony hands, which were dappled with brown spots, and as the sun reached in through the open doorway it lit up his face for the very last time and Jenna saw that there was the faintest of smiles on his old, dry lips.

chapter eight

Deeply shocked by the events of the day, Jenna wanted only to lie on her bed and sleep. Exhaustion had taken over after she had gratefully handed the responsibility to the first adult who had passed the cottage, a man she didn't know who was walking his dog. Mrs. Berry kindly closed the shop and escorted Jenna, tear stained and shaking, home to her parents. Knowing that her friend, Mr. Penrose, was dead, she felt a strange emptiness unlike anything else she had ever known, and waves of shock kept rolling over her whenever she thought of him and remembered afresh that she would never see him again.

Steve came to see her and was shown up to her room. He sat on the edge of her bed where she lay, fully clothed, with the covers pulled loosely over her.

"I know how you feel," he said gently, "I was heartbroken when my grandmother died."

"I don't think I'm heartbroken," Jenna told him truthfully, "It was just such a shock finding him like that. It wasn't as though I knew him that well, but I liked him…and I will really miss him."

"I will too. He was a curious old devil, but he knew a lot about horses, and you could tell he loved them." Steve thought about the way Mr. Penrose had always come to his gate to watch whenever horses went by, and he wished he'd made more of an effort to talk to the old man.

"I never did get to tell him about the Sand Horse," Jenna remembered suddenly and she felt tears pricking at the back of her eyes again. She tried to stop them but failed, and Steve held her in his arms for several minutes until the sobbing stopped and she grew calm again.

"I meant to tell you," he said, walking to the window and looking out. "Tufty seems a bit under the weather. He left his feed and didn't seem interested in grazing."

Jenna looked through tear soaked lashes at Steve, silhouetted against the sunlight. He had broad shoulders and was tall and very slim, being permanently on a diet to keep his weight down for racing. He cast a long shadow which stretched over her new carpet, through the open door and out on to the landing. She liked looking at him in the same way she liked looking at Gold; there was something about them both that caught her eye so it took some time for what Steve had just said to sink in.

"I don't think there's anything to worry about, but I'll keep an eye on him for you," Steve turned and smiled at her.

Jenna thought of Tufty and wondered. A strange thought came into her head.

"Do you think he knows Mr. Penrose is dead?" she asked in a whisper.

"It hardly seems likely, though it's *possible*, I suppose. There was a very close bond between the two of them and we don't really understand everything that goes on in the minds of humans and horses."

"I'll go and see him," Jenna swung her long legs to the floor and slipped her feet into her shoes.

"If you're sure you're all right," Steve looked at her anxiously.

"I'm fine. Don't fuss! You're worse than Mom," Jenna smiled and she knew she was beginning to feel a little brighter.

Tufty was listless. He stood at the gate and his eyes beseeched Jenna to take him to his stable. She was alarmed as he stumbled clumsily when he reached the cobbled yard. She made his bed around him, piling straw so high that his legs nearly disappeared. She filled his water bucket and tried to tempt him with food, but Tufty just wanted to lie down. He sank to his knees with a small groan and tried to get comfortable, but all he could think about was the gnawing, growing pain that was grumbling in his stomach. Steve watched with clouded eyes from the door, and as the first spasm of agony shook the old horse he immediately fished his phone from his pocket and keyed in the vet's number.

"Suspected colic, old pony," he said shortly to the woman who answered the call, "Green Horse Hotel, straight away if possible... thank you."

"Better see if we can get him up, Jen."

They struggled to raise Tufty to his feet.

Why give me all this straw if you won't let me lie in it? thought Tufty, infuriated, as he often was, by the strange ways of humans. The next spasm took him unaware and made his body go rigid with pain; as it eased away he turned to look at his sides, confused as to what was happening.

"He needs to walk," Steve told Jenna, trying to keep calm for her sake, as he could see the rising panic in her eyes. "You lead him. I'll get behind him and encourage him when he stops."

Jenna lost count of the number of times they walked around the yard. It was like a nightmare. It seemed incredibly cruel to be forcing her poor pony to go on when he was so weak and tired and in such pain, but she trusted Steve, and if he said Tufty had to walk, then that was what they had to make him do. It began to get dark and Steve turned on the floodlight, which was stark and glaring and painful to look

72

at. The vet arrived in a large white car. Jenna didn't recognize him.

"Terry Atkins," he introduced himself and shook both Steve and Jenna by the hand. "I'm the new guy at the practice. Sorry I'm late. I got a bit lost."

He was a fat, jolly man, with red hair and freckles. He cast an enormous shadow over Tufty who was sweating and panting, but relieved to be allowed to stand still for a while.

He got to work right away; he took Tufty's temperature, listened to his heart and to the sounds coming out of his stomach.

"It's ominously quiet in there," he said, frowning. "None of the usual plumbing noises!"

He went to his car, returned with a syringe and swiftly administered its contents into Tufty's neck.

"That should make him feel a bit more comfortable. It would help to know what started him off, though. It might give us a better idea of what we are dealing with. Has he had any changes in diet or routine?" Mr. Atkins asked.

Try as they might, neither Jenna nor Steve could come up with a single thing that might have brought on an attack of colic.

Tufty groaned again and almost fell.

"Keep him walking," Mr. Atkins voice was firm and he used his considerable weight behind Tufty to push the pony forwards.

The vet left them for another emergency with instructions to keep Tufty moving. On no account was he to be allowed to roll; there was another syringe of the anti-spasm medicine to be given if things got worse. He would, he said, come by later to see how Tufty was. His parting shot, as he folded himself awkwardly into the car, left a chill in Jenna's heart.

"We'll do our best for him, but you must remember that he

is a very, very old pony." It was not said unkindly, but it ripped at Jenna's heart.

Terry Atkins checked his watch as he turned on to the main road; he hoped he was going in the right direction to get to the farm where a cow lay injured. He made a mental note to himself to make sure he had his humane killer equipment in the car before he returned to the Green Horse Hotel.

Jenna and Steve spent most of that night walking around the yard, resting only for the brief minutes when Tufty was quiet and without pain, supporting each other with bleak, weary smiles that conveyed their unspoken determination not to give up on the old pony.

"I can't bear it if he goes like this, frightened and in so much pain," Jenna whispered through tears brought on by tiredness. "I always hoped I would just find him one sunny afternoon, in his paddock, under his favorite tree. You know, having died quietly in his sleep."

Steve had no words of comfort for her. Older, tougher, more accustomed to the sad facts of death that were part of keeping animals, he didn't feel he could properly explain the feelings that were in his head at that moment. More than anything he wanted Tufty to live, perhaps just so he could die the peaceful, gentle death that Jenna had in mind for him, perhaps because he believed deep down that all life is important and should be fought for. Or perhaps because he didn't want to see Jenna cry any more; she'd shed enough tears for one day, first for Mr. Penrose, and now for his pony who seemed to be following where his master led. At eleven o'clock the vet came again. He was very tired himself, but there was something touching about the grim determination in Jenna's eyes as she silently dared him to say the treatment wasn't working.

"We'll give him until morning, but you *must* call me if he

gets worse," he'd told her, wondering if he was right to let the pony go on suffering. The painkillers should help, he reassured himself a little later, as he turned off his bedside light. If he was honest, putting a pony to sleep was just about the last thing he wanted to do at that time of night.

Angie brought them hot coffee in a flask and sandwiches wrapped in foil. At midnight Dave came down to take Jenna's place, insisting his daughter should go and rest. Like most arguments between them, Jenna won and she was still there two hours later when Dave had finally given up and gone to bed.

"One of us might as well get some sleep," he grunted. "Good night, God bless you two... three!"

"Night, Dave," Steve answered, wishing that Jenna *would* go with him. It was obvious she was exhausted and almost asleep on her feet.

Another spasm galvanized them both into action, and Jenna felt the cold night air penetrate her befuddled head and refresh it slightly.

"Is it my imagination," she asked, "or are the pains getting less violent and coming less often?"

"They are. I've been timing them, and that's the first one he's had in twenty minutes," Steve said, hardly daring to hope that they were over the worst.

They stayed with Tufty until the first gray spears of light appeared in the sky and the birds began their wake-up call. Reassured because the last spasm had been mild and over an hour before, Jenna at last allowed herself to go to bed.

"Steve, thank you," she said. "I don't think I could have coped without you."

"You would," Steve told her. "Off you go now."

He watched as she shuffled across the yard and out through the gate.

"Goodnight, sweetheart," he called.

"Night," Jenna murmured as she turned and smiled and gave him a look that filled his heart with a strange, warm glow that he didn't really understand, but which stayed with him until he fell asleep, wrapped in a blanket in the straw next to Tufty.

✳ ✳ ✳ ✳ ✳

Jenna took two days to fully recover from her night as Tufty's nursemaid, but she didn't regret it for one moment, especially when she took him back to his paddock for the first time after his illness. She watched as he trotted stiffly away from her, then, finding his favorite place under the chestnut tree, he got down and rolled in the dappled sunshine. He wasn't very good at rolling any more and could hardly ever get all the way over, but the grass felt cool and smelled sweeter than ever after long hours in his straw bed. At that moment Tufty thought life was pretty good again.

As there had been no obvious cause for Tufty's colic, the vet had taken blood samples to test. The results would be back in a few days, but as the pony looked so much better Jenna wasn't too worried. However, the shock of finding Mr. Penrose dead and then almost losing Tufty had affected Jenna deeply. Despite feeling exhausted she found it hard to sleep, and when she did her nightmares were vivid and disturbing. She dreamed of many things, and although she could often relate them to events or discussions that she had had during the day, she could never explain why they always contained the same three elements; the sea, someone drowning and the strange, dark, woman who stood and watched and cried.

* * * * *

The new guests arrived early on Saturday morning and Jenna was only just ready for them. She had slipped back to the kitchen for breakfast, which she had to leave when she heard the truck pulling up the drive. She was greeted by three jolly, middle-aged women who, having left their husbands to look after various children, pets and businesses, were obviously determined to have a good time. They introduced themselves as Pat, Julie and Twinkle, and Jenna laughed when Twinkle, who was rather plump and very curvaceous, did a little dance, posing as a ballerina.

"I was very slim once," she told Jenna, "and so keen on dancing that my dad used to call me Twinkle toes! Somehow the name stuck."

The horses, a bay, a gray and a chestnut, came down the ramp, blinking sleepily. All three were solid, tough-looking cobs with kind outlooks and patient expressions. They reminded Jenna of the horses she had ridden at the riding school in London.

"What are their names?" she asked.

"This is Lilly," said the one called Pat who was holding the chestnut.

"And this is Gwen," Julie continued, "and Twinkle's gray is called Muffin."

Muffin, Jenna thought, was aptly named. He was easily as stout as his owner and his rump was as round and top heavy as a well-risen, freshly baked bun. She helped the ladies to settle their horses and they discussed the rides they would go on.

"I imagine you'd like to have a rest and start after lunch," Jenna said, "Dad is going to show you your rooms, then there will be coffee in the lounge," she said, trying to remember everything that Dave had told her to mention.

"Well, I'd like a quick cup of coffee," said Twinkle, "but if you two are willing, I'd rather get riding right away than wait for lunch."

There was general agreement, so Jenna took them up to the hotel to meet Dave, then went to change into her riding clothes. Her blue jodhpurs had been rained on the day before when she'd been jumping Gold in the paddock. Jenna found them in a soggy heap on the floor, so she took her best, cream riding pants out of her closet where they were hanging with her sharp, blue show-jumping jacket. Jenna looked at it wistfully and held it against her as she studied herself in the long mirror on the back of the door. When was she going to get the chance to wear it again? It seemed ages since the last time she'd jumped Gold at a show, and summer vacation was slipping by at an alarming rate. She was busy with the guests and was enjoying that most of the time, but deep down in her heart she wanted to be a show-jumper, and she knew that only hard work and lots of practice were going to get her there. She thought back to the week she had spent with Harry Houseman. She thought about all the stables she had mucked out for him and all the horses he had let her ride and the hours he had spent in the jumping paddocks shouting instructions to her as she and Gold had flown over the jumps. Jenna sighed to herself, weary all of a sudden, and weighed down by the enormity of her ambitions. Memories of finding Mr. Penrose dead flooded back to her with a jolt as they regularly did; it was still a shock to realize she would never see him again. The funeral was on Monday, and as Jenna had never been to one before she was not sure what to expect. She had asked James to come for the day to give her moral support, but he was too busy at work. She hoped she

78

wouldn't cry when she saw the coffin. She spoke to James on the phone every evening, but she found it hard to know what to say and wondered if their relationship could, or even should, go on at such a distance. Several minutes passed as she sat on the bed with her head full of thoughts. She stared at the knickknacks on the windowsill without seeing one of them, until eventually she managed to shake the mood away and get back to the day ahead. She decided to change her tee shirt, which didn't smell very fresh, as she'd done the mucking out in it. The clean black one she chose felt tight across her chest, but she liked it better than her pink one, which was the only other clean one she could find. Jenna sighed again as she pulled on her pants. They were getting tight too and she had to lie back on the bed to zip them. *That's another thing that's getting too small for me*, Jenna thought. She was used to things being too short in the legs for her, but it wasn't often that her clothes became tight around the hips and waist. I must be getting fat. She felt a slight panic rush through her. Jenna hated the skinny, straight, flat chested figure which, she felt, marked her as a child, rather than the woman she was desperate to be, but the thought of being fat was too alarming to contemplate. She stood up and studied herself again in the mirror, turning round and looking over her shoulder in an attempt to see her bottom. It wasn't an easy maneuver and Jenna tried looking through her legs, but this view was no clearer. So she got the mirror from her dressing table and rested it on the chair, adjusting it slightly until the bit she wanted was in full view. Her bottom was fatter, she decided, but, to her immense relief, her waist still seemed slim. She turned to view the whole picture from the front again. The tight pale pants accentuated her narrow, flat stomach and contrasted well with the short black tee shirt. To her surprise, the girl who looked back seemed fuller across the chest than she had remembered, with the hips and legs of a young woman, not the straight, angular lines of a boy.

"When did that happen?" she said aloud, smiling broadly and liking what she saw very much. Cramming her hair into her riding hat, she left her room and, feeling much better about herself, raced down to the stables.

Pat, Julie and Twinkle had huge amounts of energy, and Jenna found it difficult to keep up. Their appetite for long, early morning rides, followed by long afternoon rides, was boundless, and left Jenna wondering why Muffin was as stout as he was if the amount of exercise he was getting at the Green Horse Hotel was typical of his normal regime.

"Oh, yes," Twinkle replied, when Jenna asked her. "We ride all day at home. I'll do anything to get away from my husband!"

"Can we go to the beach again?" Pat asked as they set off from the yard, "We live miles from the sea so it's a real treat for us."

They clattered along the lane at a trot. Jenna found it hard not to leave the others behind, as Gold's stride was naturally long and extravagant. Pat and Twinkle, riding side by side, chatted and giggled and called back to Julie, whose mount, Gwen, was slower than the others. There were lots of places to canter, but when they walked, Jenna listened to the ladies' comments about the beauty of the countryside, and she was pleased that they were enjoying themselves. When they rounded the headland and looked out to sea, Jenna's thoughts went to Mr. Penrose and the mysterious Sand Horse, and she found it strange to think that if they ever did unravel its mystery Mr. Penrose would never know. Today the tide was high and there was no chance of seeing anything from the cliff top. Even so, Jenna halted Gold in the usual place and scanned the gray depths of the rippled water hoping to understand more. She saw nothing but the play of light on the ever-moving surface. It was a cloudy, breezy day and the beach was quiet. Jenna led her party down to the water's edge where Gold splashed and paddled and snorted at the wavelets. Lilly, Pat's mare, sidled up to him and began splashing too. Before long both riders were wet from the thighs down and laughing helplessly at the silliness of their horses. Muffin did not like water at the best of times; he was cautious by nature and skirted around puddles if he could. Never in his wildest dreams had he imagined a puddle of this magnitude, and nothing was going to persuade him to put one toe into this vast, undulating death trap.

"Have you ever swum the horses here?" Twinkle called, from where Muffin had planted himself, a little way up the beach.

"No, it's too dangerous. Further out there are some areas of very deep, soft sand," Jenna shivered as she remembered her own close encounter a few days earlier.

"I think Gold would love swimming," Pat said, "Lillie, too. Just look at them! Gold's got his nostrils under the water and Lillie's just about exhausted herself from splashing. Ohh!" She shouted suddenly, "She feels all wobbly. What's happening?"

Jenna turned in her saddle to see that Lillie, having prepared herself by splashing, was indeed wobbling as her knees began to bend and her body began to slowly sink.

"Quick," Jenna yelled, "smack her, she's going to roll!"

Julie's reactions were like lightening. She leaned across from Gwen and whacked Lillie rudely across her quarters, over and over again until the mare gave up her idea to roll and stumbled ungraciously from the water.

"That was close! With your stories of quicksand I wondered

81

what was going on for a moment or two," said Pat, rather breathless from the incident.

Jenna thought it might be a good idea to get them away from the water and headed them back up the beach at a fast canter toward the little stand that sold drinks and ice cream. As they slowed toward the top, Jenna noticed three horses heading in their direction. She watched with interest as the riders looked vaguely familiar, but it took her several seconds to realize that it was Sarah in the lead, and then a few seconds more to recognize the other two. It was Mr. and Mrs. Dixon riding Sugar and Spice. Jenna's stomach lurched slightly because she knew that in a minute their paths would cross on the narrow track, and she didn't, she really didn't, want to have to say hello to any of them.

Jenna pulled Gold on to the edge of the path and halted and Pat, Julie and Twinkle did the same. All three ladies smiled brightly at the approaching riders and said hello as they passed, but the response they got was very stony. Jenna felt herself blushing as she avoided eye contact by smoothing a stray wisp of Gold's mane over to the right-hand side. Spice stopped by Gold and stretched his muzzle toward him in recognition, but Mr. Dixon roughly jerked his head away. Jenna prayed in vain that he wasn't going to speak to her.

"I see that you are still taking money for shoddy service," he said in a loud, pompous voice. "I feel duty bound to warn you ladies that this girl can't be trusted with other people's horses. *We* had to make a formal complaint to the Tourist Association."

"Well that's odd, because we are very happy with the way Jenna has looked after us, aren't we girls?" said Twinkle, and there was hearty agreement from the others. Jenna could have kissed them all.

Mr. Dixon made a snorting noise that was supposed to

imply disbelief as he kicked Spice to move on. Mrs. Dixon rode silently past looking pointedly away from Jenna, who couldn't help but notice how tired Sugar looked as she tripped along after the others.

"Nice friendly bunch," said Pat, fully aware that the Dixons could hear her. "I presume those are the people your dad was telling us about in the bar last night."

Jenna nodded. She felt drained by the encounter. Perhaps he was right. Perhaps she wasn't capable of looking after other people's horses.

"I thought Dave must have been exaggerating," said Julie, "I didn't really believe they could be so awful."

"Take no notice of him, dear," Pat said kindly, riding alongside her. "He's just a bully. We think you are doing a terrific job. This is the best vacation I've had in ages."

When they reached the stand, Jenna offered to hold all four horses while the ladies had a coffee and sat at the picnic bench.

"We wouldn't dream of it," said Twinkle. "One of you hold Muffin for me and I'll get the drinks."

She returned a few minutes later with mugs of steaming hot chocolate and little packets of shortbread cookies for everybody.

"Keep your money in your pocket, dear, it's my treat," she told Jenna when she tried to pay her share.

Jenna couldn't help but compare these kind ladies with the dreadful Dixons. She held Gold and looked out to sea as she sipped the hot liquid. A little wave of sadness came over her as she thought of Mr. Penrose, who would never again wait for her at his garden gate, and never again stroll up to the paddock with apples for his favorite, Tufty. The funeral was the following day and Jenna was not looking forward to it. Twinkle handed Muffin's reins to Pat and

83

came over to Jenna, touching her shoulder in a gesture of support.

"Are you all right?" She asked. "Your dad told us all about the old gentleman in the village; it must have been a terrible shock for you."

Jenna nodded, not trusting herself to speak. Why was it that people being sympathetic always made her want to cry?

"I work with old people," Twinkle told her, "I'm an aide in a nursing home. I think your friend was incredibly lucky to have passed away in his own place, while he was still independent."

"It's the funeral tomorrow," Jenna took a deep breath, "I've never been to one before."

"You'll be all right. Your mom and dad will be there, won't they?"

"But what if I cry?" Jenna blurted out her worry.

"So what if you do? You won't be the only one. It's quite natural. You were fond of him and you're going to miss him. Lots of other people in the village will too. Going to his funeral is just a way of saying goodbye properly."

"Really?"

"Yes, really!" Twinkle smiled at her. "Come on now, let's have a good old gallop across the beach again. There's nothing better for putting life back into perspective."

Twinkle was right. With the wind rushing past her face and a cloud of sand and salt spray splashing up around her, Jenna was uplifted by Gold's splendor as they sped along the water's edge leaving her cares, and the other riders, far, far behind.

chapter nine

Jenna woke gasping in the night. She felt damp, and the room seemed to be spinning until the dream she had been having slowly faded and the familiar shapes of her furniture and the faintest glow of moonlight showed through the window. She looked at her clock. The green display told her that there were still several hours of night left and it made her feel lonely and a little afraid.

She had been dreaming about drowning again. This time it was Steve who had been in trouble, far out to sea in a ship that was sinking, and Jenna had been at the shore, helpless, soundlessly screaming his name. She hadn't been alone. A woman had stood beside her and offered her hand in comfort. Who was this strange woman who invaded Jenna's unconscious thoughts? A dark, sad young woman who was somehow familiar. *Which is not really surprising*, thought Jenna to herself, *as I see her nearly every night*. Shivering slightly, she got up and changed her nightgown for a dry one, then stood by the open window and looked out into the darkness. She listened, hoping she might hear an owl hoot or a fox bark, but the night was quiet except for the faint, breezy rustlings of the leaves in the trees. Then she got back into bed and forced herself to think about the day ahead of her, not wanting to close her eyes again, afraid of what she might see there.

Jenna's first feelings as the alarm went off were ones of relief. To her surprise, she had gone back to sleep quickly and slept soundly without dreaming. Then she remembered that it was the day of Mr. Penrose's funeral and her spirits sank again. She went straight to do the horses without having breakfast and found Steve already in the yard. He was handing out feeds and there was a lot of calling and stamping and maneuvering as each horse demanded to be fed first. Ears were pricked and all eyes were on Steve as he went around with buckets of mix and sugar beet to tip into their feeders.

"I'll do the hay," Jenna told him as they passed each other.

They worked well as a team. Whoever got there first fed all the horses to save any of them getting jealous, and the rest of the chores were done according to the routine Steve had established when he'd first rented the stables from Jenna's father. Feeds, hay, then mucking out for all the stabled horses. Steve had had an automatic drinking system fitted in the boxes he used, but Jenna carried water for Gold and Tufty. The three guests' horses were turned out at night, which made far less work for Jenna. She ran down to their paddock and brought them all up together and put them into stables to eat breakfast. Grooming was easy too, as the horses' summer coats were short and silky. Muffin had been rolling, and his gray coat was muddy and stained green with grass, so Jenna fetched some warm water and shampoo to remove it. She picked out their feet and body-brushed each horse, bringing a lovely shine to all except Muffin.

"Why do gray horses always find mud to roll in?" Jenna asked him.

Muffin thought this question was too silly to warrant a reply and he went on pulling at his hay net. *All* horses liked to roll in mud. Didn't Jenna know that?

"Gold doesn't get such five star treatment any more,"

Steve remarked as he passed by with a wheelbarrow on the way to the muckheap.

"Gold's not paying to stay here," Jenna retorted. "Anyway, I don't have time to do him today."

"Sorry, I forgot," Steve said, and his smile left his face. "What time is the funeral?"

"Eleven o'clock at the church. Are you coming?"

"I… I don't know…" Steve always tried to avoid funerals if he could. They reminded him of his grandmother's funeral, which had been one of the most traumatic days of his life.

"Won't James be there with you?" he asked.

"No, he couldn't get the time off work. Mom and Dad are going."

Steve glanced at his watch and did a swift calculation.

"Would it help if I went with you too?" he asked.

Jenna nodded.

"All right, I've just about got time to go home and get changed."

Everyone looked strangely formal and awkward in dark suits and coats, which didn't match the setting of the small, country church on such a bright and sunny day. People stood around in groups talking in soft tones, the birds sang and the insects buzzed, and the sounds blurred together making one noise indistinguishable from another. Dave, Angie and Jenna stood alone and slightly apart from the others. They were relatively new to the village, and although made welcome, each felt that they might be intruding on what was essentially the village's grief; a grief that they were not yet fully part of. Angie Wells thought about Jenna, thankful in her wise way that her daughter's first experience of real loss was for a man she hadn't known very long, so that although the pain was raw and genuine, it might not last too long. Dave Wells thought about his own, hectic life and wondered, morosely, if he would live to see his eighty-seventh year as Mr. Penrose had done. He wondered if he should put his arm around Jenna. Poor kid, she looked so close to tears; but he knew from experience that sympathy would only make her cry, and his daughter had always been embarrassed by her own tears. Jenna bit her lip and tried not to think about the ceremony ahead of her. She was dreading seeing the coffin, though this made no sense to her as surely this should be easier than seeing the body and she had already proved equal to that ordeal. It wasn't, though. Somehow seeing Mr. Penrose lying on the floor had been just like seeing him asleep; alive, where he belonged and protected by his own, safe home. It was the coffin that seemed so wrong for Mr. Penrose; the coffin that would take him on his last journey, down into the earth, to such a dark and alien place for a man who had loved the fields and flowers and animals so much.

The three black cars arrived almost noiselessly. Tearful ladies and serious men in tight suits got out of the first two, and in the third was the coffin, covered in flowers and beautiful in its way. Jenna hardly recognized Sheila in her sharp navy coat and dark glasses. She saw Dave take Angie's hand and squeeze it. Jenna wished Steve was there, or should it be James she was wishing for? Suddenly she heard running footsteps and Steve was by her side looking gaunt and unfamiliar in an expensive dark suit that dampened his natural *joie de vivre*.

"Would everyone go into the church now, please," asked an elderly gentleman ushering the groups toward the entrance.

Jenna stood back. She really did not want to be here. Angie looked anxious. Dave hadn't noticed.

"You go on," Steve said to Angie in a low voice, "I'll stay out here with Jen for a bit longer." If he was honest, he too was reluctant to enter the church on business such as this.

They stood against a yew tree as the procession gathered and the coffin was lifted on to the shoulders of four men, two of whom Jenna recognized from the village. They passed slowly by.

"I don't want to go in," she looked at Steve, her eyes begging him to understand.

"Nor do I, sweetheart," he said.

"But I don't want to seem disrespectful to Mr. Penrose or his family," she said, near to tears.

"They'll understand," Steve said, knowing he was right. He recalled that when his grandmother had died, most of what people did or didn't do hadn't seemed important at all. But he also remembered how small acts of kindness at the time had made a big difference. Then he had an idea.

"Let's go and get Tufty," he said, "He can be a sort of guard of honor when the coffin comes out."

Jenna thought about this strange idea, and the more she thought the less strange it became.

"Sheila would like that," Jenna said at last, "I'm *sure* she would."

They ran to Steve's car and drove quickly back to the yard.

"He's not very well groomed," Jenna groaned, brushing frantically at Tufty's tail, "but at least he's not muddy."

"There's not much time," Steve knelt down and slopped black hoof oil on the pony's feet, thinking how small they seemed compared to those of his own horses.

Jenna found a clean head collar with a new rope and they hurried the old pony down the drive and back to the village church.

"He doesn't look very funereal," Jenna commented as they stood with Tufty outside the church doors. Now that she had

89

something positive to contribute she felt much better. "I wish we'd thought of it earlier, then he could have worn a black bow or something."

Steve felt in his jacket pocket. The black suit was borrowed from his father who kept it especially for funerals, and if he knew his dad as well as he thought he did then there was a very good chance he might find a spare tie. Eric Lambert was very successful racehorse trainer, and part of his success was due to the fact that he was a man who left nothing to chance. In the depths of the pocket Steve found what he was looking for; he also found some loose change, a large blue handkerchief, and something else that made him laugh out loud despite the sober occasion – a neatly wound piece of string! He tied the tie into a loose bow and fixed it to Tufty's forelock, where it hung graceful and forlorn against his white hair.

The door of the church opened and the bearers brought the coffin out into the sunshine again. They were surprised to see the old brown and white pony whose rope was held by a very pretty young woman. Tufty lifted his head at the strange sight and watched intently as the coffin passed, and Jenna wondered if he could possibly have known how close he was to his old master. The mourners filed past, following the coffin to the graveside, and Sheila looked in bewilderment at the pony that had been her father's favorite. Her sad, red eyes filled with tears again, but as she passed Jenna she smiled her heartfelt thanks. It seemed to Jenna to be the very same smile that she had last seen on Mr. Penrose's dear, kind old face.

"Shall we follow?" Steve whispered, as the last of the congregation had passed them. "You don't have to, but I think it might help."

Jenna nodded and they drew close enough to the graveside

to hear the pastor speaking. To her surprise there were none of the somber words she'd heard on television funerals. This man seemed to be celebrating the life of Mr. Penrose, rejoicing in his contributions and talking about his body returning to the soil, the life force of the plants and animals that he had loved so much, while his spirit was freed from the ravages of old age. Jenna had never thought of it like that before. To her the grave had seemed like a dark prison, not the very basis for all new life. As the coffin was lowered into the ground her first tears came flooding silently down her face and she turned to Steve who held her close to him as he struggled with his own emotions.

"Hello," said a quiet, familiar voice behind them.

They both turned.

"James!" Jenna cried.

Steve let her go and watched as she and James kissed. He tried to see into Jenna's eyes. He wanted to know exactly what she really felt for James, but she had buried her head against his chest, and all he could see was the tender look that was in James's eyes. There was no doubt what he was feeling.

Jenna stopped crying as James smoothed her hair and held her close to him, just as Steve had done a few minutes before. James suddenly felt much older than his seventeen years.

"I'll take Tufty back now," Steve whispered, but he doubted very much that either of them heard.

chapter ten

"It was a very sweet idea of yours," Dave Wells told his daughter later, in between mouthfuls of sausage roll, "but what would you have done if he'd started to eat the floral tributes? Or worse, left a… a… well, you know, a 'present' in the churchyard?"

They were in the small back yard behind Sheila's house, which was a little less crowded than her sitting room where the buffet was laid out.

"I didn't think of that," Jenna admitted, starting to laugh at the awful possibilities. She was slightly surprised that she felt able to laugh again so soon after crying. There was a lot of laughter around her and that was another thing that she found surprising. Apparently it was all right to laugh at a funeral after all. She said as much to her mother who was sitting on a wooden bench sharing a bowl of potato chips with James.

"Of course, hon. Mr. Penrose wouldn't have wanted anyone to be sad, any more than you or I would."

Jenna felt light inside for the first time in days, which must be due, she thought to herself, to the relief of having gotten through the funeral. Perhaps James turning up unexpectedly might have had something to do with it too. She smiled at James as he sat talking to her mother and thought how handsome he looked in his suit. Whenever he was with her she could hardly believe that she ever doubted they should be together. It was the fact that they spent so much time apart that was the real problem, she thought.

James didn't ever have doubts about Jenna. It seemed to him that when he wasn't with her he just loved her all the more. Normally an honest young man, it was a sure indication of his feelings for her that he had been able to lie quite convincingly to his boss on the phone that morning, feigning a severe bout of stomach flu. He had tried to phone her when he'd gotten stuck in traffic, but didn't really expect her to have her cell phone switched on during a funeral. When he'd turned up late and found her in Steve's arms his heart had plummeted. He was all too aware that Jenna had once had feelings for Steve. What he wasn't sure about and would love to know was what were Steve's feelings for Jenna? He decided to take things as they seemed on the surface and be thankful to Steve that he had been there to comfort Jenna until he, James, had arrived to take his rightful place at her side. He sipped at his lemonade, and hoped he had been nodding in all the right places, but suspected that he hadn't as Angie was now looking at him with an amused smirk on her face.

"Shall we go?" Jenna slipped her hand into his as she took her mother's place beside him on the bench.

"Where, back to your place? I've got to get the car back to Mom tonight, but I don't have to start back for a couple of hours," James told her, thinking how stunning she looked in her simple blue sundress.

"My ladies have gone for a ride by themselves today," she told him, "so I'm free for the afternoon. Maybe we could go somewhere."

"We could go and have some lunch, and then have a walk," James said, thinking how nice it would be to show Jenna off.

93

They left Dave and Angie chatting and went back through the house to find Sheila to say goodbye.

"Thank you so much for coming, Jenna, and thank you for bringing Tufty. Dad would have loved to know he was there," her eyes filled with tears again. "Dad was very fond of you, you know."

"I was fond of him too," Jenna's throat felt tight and painful as she tried hard to keep her tears at bay.

"He left you something. He asked me to give it to you the day before he died, but I forgot to take it to work with me. Here, it's in a box somewhere," Sheila's head disappeared into a cupboard by the front door. "Here you are. I've no idea what it is. Some old horsy stuff, knowing him."

She handed Jenna a cardboard box. Inside was a cookie tin sealed up with lots of brown sticky tape.

"Oh, er... thank you," Jenna was touched and a little taken aback. It was odd to be receiving a gift from someone who wasn't alive any more. "I'll let you know what's in it."

She carried the package carefully out to the car. James held the door open for her and his heart swelled with pride. Surely, the prettiest girl in the whole world was coming out to lunch with him!

Jenna was very quiet and thoughtful during the days that followed Mr. Penrose's funeral. It wasn't that she was sad exactly; more bewildered by the realization that life was so fragile and could stop at any moment.

Angie was concerned. It wasn't like Jenna to dwell on things, and it wasn't as if she had been very close to Mr. Penrose. Dave was concerned too, but his thoughts, at the height of the summer season, were otherwise occupied, and he never had understood the complexities of what he saw to be the woman's mind, his daughter's least of all. Of all the people close to Jenna, Steve understood her best. Having lost his grandmother when he was Jenna's age, he could remember only too clearly the shock of realizing that things didn't just go on the same forever and ever. He guessed that Jenna knew for the first time the complete finality of death and was relating it to herself and her own family. He left her alone because he felt that was what she wanted, but he made it clear that he was there if she needed him, and Jenna was grateful.

It was James who was most affected by Jenna's uncharacteristic pensiveness. Separated from her by many miles, and missing her badly, he blew it up out of all proportion and became beside himself with worry. Worry that this unfamiliar, introspective Jenna might be losing interest in him. Worry that he might lose her. Just worry, as only a young man in love can worry, when he is parted from his girlfriend, helpless, and with too much time to think. After three days of awful phone calls, when he rambled on senselessly to fill the long pauses when it was Jenna's turn to speak, James could stand it no longer. He walked out of his job at the bookshop and went home to pack, hoping that his boss had once been young and in love and would therefore understand. He got a lift to the station and was waiting in the yard when Jenna got home from a day's trek with Pat, Julie and Twinkle. He had made himself useful and prepared the feeds and filled up the hay nets, so all that the weary riders had to do was untack their horses, and he was even gallant enough to help with that.

"Your young man can come and work for me any time," Twinkle called to Jenna as James carried her saddle to the tack room.

"Shall I take your horses to the paddock for you?" James offered. "Then you can get yourselves some tea."

"How very kind," said Julie. "I could do with a drink."

"You're just trying to get rid of us so you can have Jenna to yourself," laughed Twinkle. "Come on, girls, let's get out of the way!"

They walked stiffly up the path to the hotel, and as their voices grew faint, the peace of the stable yard was once more restored with just birdsong and the gentle sounds of horses eating to break the silence.

James stood looking at Jenna and feeling awkward. His hands were full of leading ropes, but the three tired horses stood patiently.

"I didn't know what else to do," he told her quietly. "Tell me to go away if you want to."

"Why should I do that? I'm really pleased to see you. It was just a bit of a surprise, that's all," Jenna's voice was flat, and she felt exhausted as she held his gaze, wondering why she didn't feel happier.

"You don't *sound* very pleased."

"I'm just tired. Come on, let's get the horses finished. I need a bath and something to eat. I'll probably feel better after that."

"I'm borrowing a boat from a friend of your dad's," James announced to Jenna when she came down for breakfast the next morning.

James was sitting alone in the kitchen with a pile of toast and a newspaper; Dave and Angie had long since started work. There was an empty coffee cup on the table and Jenna smiled to herself. Her dad left coffee cups in the same way that a snail left a shiny trail.

"I didn't know my dad had any yacht-owning friends," said Jenna, surprised.

"Ah, well, when I said boat, I meant more of a dinghy, a small inflatable one that fits in the trunk of a car. I'm going to get it later."

"And what do you want a boat for?" Jenna asked as she buttered some toast.

"To look for your Sand Horse, of course," said James. "I thought you'd want to get to the bottom of the mystery."

Jenna thought about this for a while as she munched on her toast without tasting it. Would she really like to know what the Sand Horse was? Part of her did, but there was another part that shied away from it, frightened of what it might be. *I'm beginning to sound like Mr. Penrose*, she thought sadly. *I mustn't think like that. Of course the horse is real. We've both seen it, and the sooner the mystery is cleared up the better*, she told herself sternly.

"I've been thinking," James told her, his eyes shining with enthusiasm, "the horse must be a very long way out, which means it will only be visible during very low tides. It would be too dangerous to try to find it on foot because of the sands, but a boat would be safe enough. I've done a bit of diving. I could anchor up and see what I could find out."

"And Dad thinks this is a good idea, does he? He must if he's fixed you up with a dinghy," Jenna said skeptically.

"Well, I didn't actually tell him what I wanted it for, just that I thought you could use some fun, and that a bit of boating might be one way of getting it."

"It wouldn't be fair to worry him," Jenna said with a grin.

"I knew you'd see it like that," said James, basking in the warmth of her smile.

"We could go tomorrow afternoon," said Jenna, suddenly feeling a faint sense of excitement stealing through her. "Twinkle and the ladies are leaving in the morning and there aren't any other guests booked for a couple of days."

"Tomorrow it is, then," said James, glad that he could do something to please her.

Jenna was genuinely sad to say goodbye to her guests.

"It's been the best vacation we've ever had," Julie told her. "We'll definitely come back next year."

"You've been marvelous," said Twinkle, "I don't know how you've put up with us three chattering away all day long!"

"I've enjoyed it," said Jenna, "You've been great company," she added, and they could tell that she really meant it.

"We bought you these," Pat handed her a bag, "If they don't fit you can change them."

Jenna recognized the bag. It came from Coopers, the local saddle shop. Inside she found a beautiful pair of riding pants. They were pale blue with a dark blue suede seat for extra grip, the very expensive sort that Jenna had been wanting for ages.

"I don't know what to say! They're stunning and just what I need – the right size, too. Thank you so much!"

Jenna waved and waved as their truck moved slowly from the yard.

"I wonder why the Dixons didn't buy me a present," she said to James, with more than a hint of sarcasm in her voice.

"I imagine they just forgot," he told her, laughing, "They'll send it to you when they realize their mistake! Come on, we've got a mystery to solve."

The first hunt for the Sand Horse was great fun, but not at all successful. James borrowed Angie's car, and he and Jenna drove to Rush Bay and spent a very long and exhausting time blowing up the inflatable dinghy in the parking lot. They took turns working the inefficient foot pump, and both got bored of the exercise long before the little boat looked any firmer than a week-old balloon.

"I wonder if your Mom has a better pump in her car," James said, straightening up and going to look. "This is more like it!"

With the help of an electric pump, plugged into the car battery, they were soon on their way, carrying the now much larger dinghy between them.

"We'll have to climb down the cliff path to get to the right place," Jenna told him. "If we try from the other side of the beach the lifeguards will stop us."

The sea was very flat and calm and although the day was overcast, there were still a lot of vacationers sitting on the far side of the beach. James saw them as little dots and splashes of color on the warm brown sand.

"When the tide is higher, this part of the beach is cut off," Jenna told him, "but you can always climb the cliff path, so it isn't dangerous, just a bit steep."

They scrambled wetly into the dinghy, splashing each other and giggling, and almost overturning the little craft.

"Be sensible," James shouted in his best school principal's voice, but Jenna, feeling happy again, wouldn't let go of her carefree mood and rocked and splashed James even more.

James rowed strongly up and down a short stretch of water, keeping parallel with the shore at about the place Jenna thought she had seen the mysterious horse. They looked down into the clear water, scanning the sandy bottom for any sign of the horse, but saw only stones and seaweed and the silver glint of tiny fish.

Jenna sat up and stared toward the cliff, trying to calculate the distance from the shore and the exact position they were searching for.

"Maybe it moves with the tides," suggested James.

"I don't think it can, or it would have been washed away long before now. I think it's probably further out than this. I'd need to be standing on the cliff again to be sure."

James scanned the horizon and noted the dark clouds gathering.

"Let's come back tomorrow and have another try. I'm getting cold," he looked at his wet shirt and shot an exaggerated angry look across to Jenna, "because *somebody* thought it would be funny to soak me!"

They rowed back to the shore and carried the dinghy between them up the steep cliff path. They were both exhausted by the time they reached the top. James tied the boat to the car's roof rack to save them having to deflate and re-inflate it later.

"Tomorrow," Jenna said as he sat down in the driver's seat beside her, "tomorrow, I'll ride Gold here and meet you. Then I can stand in exactly the same place and be the same height and everything as I was when I first saw it. We could use our phones and I can direct you to the right place."

"Good idea," said James, thinking how pretty she looked with her hair wet and sandy and her cheeks flushed pink from exercise. It was lovely to see her looking so cheerful. He stretched and yawned lazily, feeling so relaxed in her company. *We're just like we were before Mr. Penrose died*, he thought to himself, happily. Then he remembered something.

"I keep forgetting to ask. What was in that package that Sheila Penrose gave you after the funeral?"

Jenna stiffened visibly in her seat. The package. Jenna had been trying to forget about the package, though goodness only knew why it was causing her so much anxiety. It was still stowed out of sight under her bed where she had put it several days before. How she wished Sheila had remembered to give it to her before her father had died. Then she could have opened it with interest and enjoyment and thanked the old man and discussed whatever it was with him in person. Instead, it lay in her room like a brooding presence, which for the last few hours she had managed to forget.

"I don't want to talk about it," she said in a small, sad

voice, and she seemed to shrink back into her pensiveness like a flower closing its petals at dusk.

James drove home in silence, wishing vainly that he could turn the clock back two minutes so that he could keep his big mouth shut.

chapter eleven

Waking the next morning to sunshine did a great deal to restore Jenna's good mood and promote a sense of reality about the things she was worried about. The raw shock of finding Mr. Penrose dead was fading and the sadness was leaving her too as she began to see that what everyone had been telling her was true. He had had a very long and happy life and a quick, peaceful death in his own home, which was what he would have wished for. If only she could find the courage to open the package. She didn't even know what was stopping her. What could be so awful about a gift from a friend? It was probably a bit of old harness that once had belonged to Tufty, or perhaps some grooming kit he'd found in his shed. He had once given her a strange brush of brass links, which he said he'd used for years to burnish a glorious shine on the summer coats of the working horses he'd looked after. She had tried to use it once, but Gold had objected to the hard feel of it on his soft, Thoroughbred skin, so it was at the back of a cupboard somewhere gathering dust.

"I'll open it now," she spoke out loud to make the words mean more.

She knelt down and felt beneath her bed. Her hands found the hard, cool tin and she shivered involuntarily.

"Jenna, breakfast's ready," she heard her father call from the kitchen.

"I'll do it later," she promised herself, relieved.

An hour later when she was riding along a quiet lane on the way to Rush Bay, Jenna found her head crammed full of thoughts. Gold, allowed to amble along at his own pace, realized that she was not paying attention and took full advantage of the situation. Well-mannered horses did not nibble at the hedgerows; it was one of the first things he had learned and it was a very tough rule to keep, tempted as he was in the summer months by the lush, fragrant greenery. He could feel Jenna's hand lightly on his rein and sensed that whatever she was thinking about, it certainly wasn't him. It was worth a try; first he snatched slyly at some overhanging grasses, scattering the seed heads and making his nose tickle. When this misdemeanor was ignored he tried a bolder move, and momentarily slowed his pace to grab a really juicy mouthful of sweet, wild barley. The reprimand, if it came, would be worth it, but it didn't come and he munched the delicacy as he strolled thoughtfully along. It was easy to eat the long stalks with his new bridle, much easier than when he'd had a cold, hard lump of metal in his mouth. Lulled into a lovely sense of security by what he took to be Jenna's total change of heart about his snacking from the hedgerows, Gold finally overstepped the mark when, emboldened by his earlier successes, he stopped at a gateway and reached his head down to graze at an irresistibly lush, green swath of grass. The reins were snatched roughly from Jenna's hands and she returned from her mental wanderings with a shout of anger and a tap with her crop across her horse's shoulder. Gold was left with no doubt; the rules hadn't changed, but he wondered in a hurt, reproachful way about the inconsistency of people, Jenna in particular.

James was enjoying himself. The early morning sun was pleasant on his back and the gentle, incoming tide was easy to row his little boat across, despite the extra weight of half a concrete block, which he had collected from the beach and intended to use for an anchor. From time to time he looked up to the cliff, expecting Jenna at any moment, but mostly he stared down into the shallow waters at the tide-rippled sands that seemed to shift beneath his craft.

Everything was beautiful about the day, the salty smell of the sea, the cries of the seagulls and the heavenly twittering of the airborne skylarks, the lapping of the water as it caressed the boat and the diamonds that twinkled and sparkled on the surface of the clear waters. *Everything is just perfect*, James thought to himself, with a deep, contented sigh. The next time he looked up he saw the silhouette of a fine horse on the cliff top with Jenna in the saddle looking down at him. His cell phone chirped foolishly, and the timeless, ageless magic of the moment was lost to the harsher, modern world.

"Hi, Jen. Did you have a good ride over?"

"Lovely, thanks. Have you found anything?"

"No, can you see anything?"

"No. I'll ride along a bit and call you back."

The path was crumbly in places and Gold had to step carefully. Trusting him, Jenna stared out across the water, willing the shadowy shape of the horse to become clear to her. There was nothing to see. For a brief moment Jenna wondered if old Mr. Penrose had been right to be scared. Perhaps there was some sinister, ancient magic attached to the sightings of the Sand Horse. Perhaps it only became visible to certain people at certain times. *Vulnerable, susceptible people*, she thought to herself and a shiver shot through her, leaving her wondering why she wanted to see it again.

Three times she turned Gold and retraced her steps, but still she saw nothing.

"It's no good," she told James, struggling to manage Gold

with one hand as she held the phone to her ear with the other. "Maybe the tides are wrong or something. Gold's getting restless. I think I'll go and give him a run across the sands, if you don't mind."

"I'll stay and look a bit longer," James told her. "I've always loved messing around in boats."

Jenna was aware that James was watching her as she rode across the headland, and that he would most probably wait for her to come back into sight at the top of the beach to see her gallop across the sand. She pulled her stirrups up four holes and adjusted her balance as she trotted on, hovering above the saddle, picking a route along the water's edge away from the scattered, early morning vacationers. Steve had taught her to ride safely across wet sand. She knew that she should canter slowly at first, looking ahead for holes, deep puddles or soft areas which could bring a fast horse down. Only on the way back could they gallop; the trick was to follow Gold's hoof prints, retracing the line that she knew to be free from dangers.

The beach was long and Jenna trotted and cantered for several minutes before steadying the now blowing Thoroughbred and walking him in a wide circle to get his breath back. *Mine too*, she thought ruefully. Her legs had tired quickly from the shortened stirrups and she kicked her feet free and stretched. She looked for James. The bright orange dinghy showed up clearly as a tiny speck of warm color in a cool blue sea. She couldn't see James, though. Perhaps he was stretched out in the bottom of the boat, sunbathing. Turning her attentions back to Gold she ran her hand down his damp, steaming neck and listened for his breathing, which was back to its normal, slow rhythm. Her own heart started to beat a little faster in anticipation of the gallop back which was always wild and at an unbelievable speed, her sensations heightened by the rush of the salty sea air. Gold knew what was coming next, and he danced on the spot as Jenna got her stirrups back and turned him in the direction of home. He shot forward like the racehorse he was meant to have been and stretched down into his bridle, snatching the sweaty reins from Jenna's fingers. Gold galloped strongly down the beach, leaning slightly on Jenna's contact. With a smile on her face and pride and fear running through her veins Jenna cast her eyes sideways to look at their running shadow, stretched and distorted by the angle of the sun. At the sound of drumming hooves, people stopped and turned to watch the magnificent chestnut horse and his young rider as they flew along, splashing through the wet sand, showering gritty droplets into the air. All who watched her pass wondered what it must feel like to be Jenna at that moment, riding so swiftly on her glorious horse.

Flushed, hot and sweaty, despite wearing only a tee shirt, Jenna slowed to a walk and turned Gold toward the shallow waters where she let him splash and play in the cooling, rippled waves.

She looked for James again, certain that this time he'd be looking out for her, but though she was much nearer, and could see the dinghy clearly, there was no sign of him. Suppressing a little icicle of fear, she pulled her phone from her jodhpur pocket and keyed in his code.

"Answer it, James," she pleaded.

Jenna stared at the orange splash that was the dinghy until her eyes hurt. How far away was it? One hundred yards? Two hundred yards? She urged Gold forward into the water and stood high in her stirrups, hoping against hope that she would see James rise sleepily in the boat. Answering the urgent squeezes from Jenna's legs, Gold walked on. The water was over her boots now and the chill took her breath away. Gold lifted his head higher as the water got deeper, but when it lapped over his back the laws of nature took over and he found himself swimming strongly toward the boat. Jenna hardly knew what had happened. As soon as Gold struck out with his forelegs she was lifted from the saddle and would have floated away from him if she hadn't grabbed his mane. She wasn't riding her swimming horse. There was no way she could sit on the saddle; instead, she was being dragged behind him, guiding him lightly toward the little orange boat. She had never felt so scared in all her life, or so alone. The seabed seemed to be yards below, and with every stroke they were leaving the safety of the land behind them. Gold's breathing was a loud, snorting, rasping bark, which unnerved her. Was he breathing water? Or was it just the strange angle at which he had to hold his head? Jenna clung desperately to Gold's mane, pulling herself closer to his body, but the water was taking her, and it took all her strength to stop her legs from floating backwards. As they neared the empty dinghy, Jenna's worst fears were confirmed. Where was James? How could he have disappeared so completely? Feeling Gold turning for the shore again, Jenna pushed away from him and launched herself at the dinghy, holding desperately to the wet, slippery side for a few seconds before scrambling inside.

"James," she screamed, "James, where are you?"

The boat was tethered to the spot by a rope, which ran taught and straight down into the water. Jenna leaned over the side and was sickened by what she saw. A dark shape was thrashing desperately, submerged about two yards beneath the boat. Jenna jumped into the water and within moments she was beside James. Sand and bubbles swirled around them, and she could hardly see what was happening, but what she could see confused her. Unbelievably, the anchor rope was tied tightly around James' wrist and, thrash and struggle as he would, he couldn't free himself. Panic was rising within Jenna. How long had James been down here? How much longer could he hold his breath? How much longer could she hold hers? She traced the rope down to where it was tied around a concrete block on the seabed and, with one hand, she pulled James toward her, lessening the tension. With the other hand she struggled with the knot, forcing her fingers to grip and pull until, to her overwhelming relief, the rope came free from the block. James shot away from her, bursting through the surface of the water and into the safe blueness above. A split second later she was beside him, and she supported him as they both clung to the side of the dinghy. James's face was white and his breathing was loud and rasping. Air tore into his body in great gulps and, as Jenna watched, terrified, he coughed and spluttered and retched. Slowly his color began to return to normal and he dragged himself into the boat and lay quietly as Jenna rowed slowly back to the shore.

"Thanks," he said at last.

"Are you all right?"

"I think so. My chest feels like a car's driven over it, but apart from that, there's no damage done."

"What happened?"

There was a long silence and she watched James's face, noting the strange color of his skin and the look of deep shock and fear in his eyes.

"I think I found the horse," he said at last. "I was just about to call it a day when I spotted a shape when the sun went behind a cloud for a few moments. So I dropped my 'anchor,' a lump of concrete I'd found on the beach, and dived down to investigate. The trouble was, I couldn't keep myself at the bottom long enough to get a really good look. I kept bobbing back up to the surface. I was diving for ages. I went down so many times but I was just getting tired. I could see you approaching and I really wanted to be able to tell you I'd found it for sure. So, the next time I dived under, I did a really stupid thing."

"You tied yourself to the anchor rope? Under two yards of water?" Jenna was incredulous.

"Not exactly, I tied a loop in it and slipped my wrist through. But then a wave moved the boat and the loop pulled tight. I panicked. I just couldn't free myself."

James leant his head in his hands and his voice was barely a whisper, "I might have drowned," he said.

"You almost did," Jenna told him. "If Gold hadn't brought me to you then you would have."

Gold! Jenna dropped her oars and turned to scan the shore. In her worry about James she had completely forgotten about Gold.

"It's all right, he's over there," James was pointing. "Some girls have got him. It looks as though they're feeding him their sandwiches."

"He deserves a sandwich after what he did for you today," Jenna smiled at James and her heart filled with a strange softness as she took in his salty, sticky hair and his ashen, tear-stained face. She had nearly lost him. Really, really lost him, and lost him forever. With this unbearable thought came tears, but she fought them back as she rowed resolutely to the shore.

Sitting in the hotel garden with the evening sun filtering gently through the leaves of a sycamore tree, Jenna sat and sipped at a tall glass of iced orange juice. It seemed a very long way from the frightening events of the morning on the beach and, apart from feeling tired, she had just about gotten over the shock. She wasn't sure if James had, though. He had been very quiet all through supper, and he wasn't talking now. She could guess what was going through his mind, or she thought she could. It didn't take a genius to imagine how a near-death experience would occupy your thoughts completely. He had already made her promise not to tell anyone. *Poor thing*, she thought, *he must be going over and over it in his head, beating himself up for doing such a stupid thing.*

"Are you all right?" She said at last.

"Me?" James sounded surprised, "Of course, never better."

"You mustn't be too hard on yourself," she said with a wicked smile, "I mean anyone could make a silly mistake like that. I'm always tying myself to lumps of concrete at the bottom of the sea, I just can't help myself sometimes!"

For a long time, James stared at her and said nothing, but there was a reassuring twinkle in his eyes.

"I wasn't thinking about that," he told her aloofly, "I was trying to work out a way, a *safe* way, to get that horse to the surface once and for all."

Jenna was genuinely shocked.

"You mean you want to go back there and do it all again? You're mad, completely, raving mad. Don't think I'm coming with you. I've had enough of the Sand Horse – Mr. Penrose was right, there are some things that are just best left alone."

The anger rose like a storm within her and she jumped from her chair and raced away. She didn't want James to see her crying. She always seemed to be crying these days, she thought sadly to herself as she made her way down to the paddock where Gold and Tufty were turned out for the night. She always felt a magnetic attraction to the horses whenever she felt sad. They were standing, nose to tail, in the shade of the rough, high hedge, nodding gently to disturb the flies that were the bane of their lives during the height of the summer weeks. She buried her face in Tufty's mane and sniffed his familiar, horsy smell, which was more wonderful to her than any perfume she had come across so far in her life. Then she went to Gold's head and scratched him behind the ears in the exact spot that he loved the most, and he leaned against her hand and twisted his head round to enjoy it all the more. Jenna laughed and scratched him until her fingers ached.

"You are filthy," she told him, examining her hands, which had turned gray and greasy.

Gold blew into Jenna's hair, but it tickled his nose and made him snort loudly, which woke Tufty with a start from his doze.

Jenna laughed and realized with relief how much happier she felt.

"Good night, you two," she said as she patted their round, shiny rumps and went to find James to say sorry for getting mad.

chapter twelve

It was after midnight, and it had been a long and very tiring evening. As Dave Wells wandered wearily through reception on his way to lock the office for the night, he was thinking only of his bed. The telephone rang just as he was passing it and he jumped at the intrusive, plaintive sound that pierced through the tranquil, bedtime atmosphere of the sleepy hotel. Dave glanced at the clock. Half past twelve. *If that's someone wanting to book a table in the restaurant, I'll scream*, he thought to himself.

"Green Horse Hotel, *night* porter speaking," Dave said, unable to resist the sarcasm. It was amazing how some people just assumed that because you ran a hotel you never went to sleep!

"Mr. Wells, is that you?" The lady's voice was familiar and she sounded very anxious.

"Yes, this is Dave Wells, how can I help?"

"It's Sarah, Sarah Sheldon. I'm so sorry to call you. If there was anyone else I could turn to, believe me I would. I need Jenna's help. I have four horses with colic; two of mine and two boarders. The vet's here but we can't cope alone… I know we've had our differences…"

"Four?" Dave was shocked, remembering the effort it had taken to nurse Tufty, one very small pony, through his illness.

"The vet says it's viral. Others may come down with it yet. I can't contact the owners. They won't answer their cell

112

phone; asleep, I imagine. I don't care about them, but I do care about their horses…" Sarah's voice became low and flat as weariness hit her. "It was just a thought about Jenna, but I can understand if you don't want to wake her…"

Dave Wells could hear that Sarah was at the end of her rope. His wife and daughter were fond of telling him that he could be obstinate and pig-headed, but he wasn't the sort to bear a grudge or to refuse a helping hand to a damsel in distress.

"It's all right, Sarah, we'll be with you as soon as humanly possible," was all he said before he put the phone down.

That night was one of the strangest, and, in some ways, scariest that Dave had ever spent, unused as he was to the close proximity of large, panicking horses who were thrashing around in pain. As soon as they got there he was handed the rope of the smallest of the sick animals, Rosy, one of Sarah's ponies from the riding school.

"Keep her walking, whatever else you do," was the curt instruction from the weary young vet in charge.

James was given a tall, gray gelding and Jenna a chestnut mare who she immediately recognized as Mrs. Dixon's Sugar. *And that's Spice*, she thought, looking across at James as they began the relentless, weary trudging around the yard, which, after medicine had been administered, was the best way to prevent the horses rolling in their agony and damaging themselves irreparably.

Dave circled the yard, coaxing his reluctant pony forward with kind words and pats. The work was wearying, coming as it did at the time when his body expected to be tucked into bed and fast asleep. *But if the kids can do it, then so can I*, Dave told himself as he caught James's eye across the yard and exchanged a rueful smile.

Jenna was having the worst of it. Spice and Rosy were not

too badly affected and were willing to walk, but Sugar was having agonizing spasms that racked her body and sent her first into a rigid trance-like state, and then to a plunging panic as she tried desperately to free herself from the awful pains inside her. Jenna held on grimly to the rope and soothed the terrified mare with words when she could. But the dangers of rolling were very real, and at the first signs of the mare going down Jenna had to shout at her to move, pummeling her puny fists into the big mare's sweating sides. She hated doing it, but she must not let her sink to the ground where her contortions could twist her bowels and end her life.

Dave discovered a new respect for his daughter, whose toughness and spirit were like a shining beacon of energy, as she battled to move her patient who seemed so huge and dangerous compared to Jenna. He discovered that, when stressed, she used words that he hadn't realized were in her vocabulary, and more than once he wondered what his wife would have said if she had been there to hear her. In the middle of the night, at his lowest ebb when he was more than ready to give up, Dave looked across at Jenna and could have cried with love as he saw in her eyes her passion for horses and her determination that Sugar was not going to die. Jenna wasn't giving up and he wouldn't either, so on he trudged, encouraging his reluctant, shuffling pony to make the effort that would, with luck, save her life.

In one of the stables at the end of the yard lay the fourth patient, who was past walking, and Dave could hear Sarah and the vet talking in sober, whispered tones. When the sharp crack of the humane killer rang out through the still night air he wasn't really surprised, but that didn't stop the tears from streaming down his face as he cried quietly in the dark. He wondered if this awful night was ever going to end.

James spent the whole night working on autopilot. Only his body was trudging around in endless circles, helping the awful woman who had been so rude to him at the show. His head was back at the hotel, fast asleep. He wasn't his best in the middle of the night, being the sort of person who needed his sleep, and he was doing what he was doing for the sake of the horses, and because Jenna had asked him to. He had said very little when Jenna had woken him, though there was plenty he would have liked to say. She implored him to hurry and get dressed quickly as she stood at the door and keyed in Steve's number to her cell phone.

"He's not answering; I bet he's let the batteries go dead. He's such an idiot sometimes," she said with disgust.

Not such an idiot, James thought wryly, but he was very pleased that, for once, Jenna considered Steve so.

Jenna had little time to think about what she was doing, so anxious was she for the safety of the kindly chestnut mare, which she had grown fond of during the short time she'd been at the hotel. She tried to block out the thought that Sugar was even worse than Tufty had been and how very close they had come to losing him. *Sugar is much younger*, she kept telling herself, but as the night wore on there came a dull glazed look to the mare's eyes that tore at Jenna's heart.

"Don't give up," she whispered to Sugar, "please, don't give up."

"I think we'll risk another shot of this stuff. Hold her still, please," the young vet said, clearly not enjoying himself. He'd lost one of his patients, and now this one seemed to be deteriorating too. A fifty per cent success rate wasn't exactly great. He began to prepare the speech in his head, the one he hated most about how it wasn't fair to let an animal go on suffering. He glanced sideways at Jenna and thought her pretty and tough and wondered how she would take the loss

115

after all her hard work. Jenna knew he was looking at her, and by some strange intuition she knew what he was thinking. She turned and fixed him with her clear, honest eyes and held his gaze for several seconds.

"Another hour," she demanded, and she coaxed the mare forward.

The vet nodded and smiled to himself. He was under Jenna's spell and would have agreed to anything. *What a beautiful girl,* he thought, his heart a little lighter as he went to check the other horses.

Jenna wasn't sure why she had asked for another hour. She could see the hopeless look in Sugar's eyes, and she knew that the mare was giving in to the pain but, tired as she was, Jenna wasn't ready to let her go. Sarah brought her a mug of hot chocolate and passed it to her with a whispered thanks and a look that repaired all the hurt that passed between them.

"How is that lovely show-jumper of yours?" Sarah asked as she walked with the girl at Sugar's head.

"He's fine, but I haven't had much time for competitions recently."

"That's a shame. You could be good, very good, in fact." Sarah thought back to all the keen young show-jumpers she had ever taught; few had had Jenna's talent and even fewer her steely determination.

Jenna felt her phone vibrating in her pocket and took it out, cutting its thin, incongruous tone with a stab of her thumb.

"Jenna, it's Steve. I missed your call, is everything all right?"

"Steve, thank goodness!" She felt relief flood through her as she quickly told him what had happened.

"He's coming to help," Jenna announced happily, somehow

sure that his being there would make everything better. Her brightness cut through James's heart as if she had stabbed him. Was he ever going to feel that Jenna was really his? Or would Steve always be there to overshadow him?

By the time the first red streaks of daylight scored the sky, Rosie and Spice had both been returned to their stables and were tentatively pulling at a few strands of hay. So far, none of Sarah's other horses were showing any signs of colic and Dave had returned home with a reluctant James, who was dead on his feet.

Jenna was walking with her eyes shut, so familiar was the path she trod. She had refused all offers of relief, as she was determined to see the task through to whatever the end might bring.

"I'll open my eyes when the sun gets over the horizon," she whispered to Sugar, "and when it does, you'll feel better."

But this milestone came and went and the dullness didn't leave the chestnut mare's eyes and the spasms still wracked her body at regular intervals.

"Steve will be here soon. He'll bring some luck with him and you'll feel better then," Jenna promised, but she was running out of optimism.

Jenna's exhaustion was so complete that her thoughts were almost dream-like, and though she was still walking she was probably sleeping too. She missed the sound of Steve's car pulling up outside the yard and hardly noticed as he picked her up and carried her easily into Sarah's kitchen where he put her in an armchair and covered her with a blanket from the dog's basket. Somewhere in her dreams she knew that before he had left her he had bent and kissed her forehead. She opened one weary eye and watched him as he slipped quietly out of the kitchen door. How she wished it had been her lips. She smiled to herself and let her mind drift off to peaceful, more magical places.

"Sandwich, Jen?" Steve balanced a plate carrying a peanut butter sandwich on the arm of the chair where she sat.

Slowly Jenna uncurled herself and stretched her legs carefully in a way that reminded Steve of a sleepy cat.

"What time is it?" She asked.

"Half past twelve. You've been snoring for ages!"

"I don't snore… do I?" Jenna looked distastefully at the blanket on her knees, and then rose and put it gingerly back in the dog basket.

Memories of the night came suddenly to her.

"Sugar… is she… is she dead?"

"No. She's hanging on, not right yet, but a bit brighter. The vet has stopped talking about destroying her. He won't say for certain that she's definitely going to make it, but I know he thinks she will."

"Have the Dixons been to see her?"

"Yes. Mrs. Dixon was in floods of tears and Mr. Dixon was his usual charmless self, threatening to sue Sarah for negligence. Luckily the vet was here at the time and he put them well and truly in their place by telling them that neither of their horses would be alive if it wasn't for Sarah, and you and James. Dave too, of course."

Jenna munched on her sandwich without really tasting it. Her thoughts were absorbed by the events of the night before, which had now taken on a distant, confused quality, and she was unsure which bits she had dreamt and which were for real. She sighed, but it was a happy, contented sigh. The details weren't important. All that mattered was that Sugar was getting better and that she was friends with Sarah again.

Three days later Jenna was back at Sarah's yard, this time with Gold and James. They were all in the paddock and James was self-appointed course builder, adjusting and moving the jumps, while Sarah concentrated on Jenna's approach and position. For Jenna this was pure heaven. For the first time in ages, she really felt as though she was progressing, moving forward with her riding and getting nearer to her dreams. Jumps came and went under the powerful chestnut as Jenna practiced her corners and angles, shaving seconds off her time around the course. Gold was behaving surprisingly well and Sarah was full of praise for the pair of them.

"I suppose you'll be competing at Redchester at the end of the month?"

"I'm not sure," Jenna answered. "It's our busiest time. We've got riders booked in over that weekend and anyway, I haven't got any transportation. I can hardly ride to Redchester even if I did have the time."

"You ought to get your Dad to sponsor you. Then he could buy you a trailer and charge it to the business," said Sarah. She had just about forgiven Dave Wells for stealing her idea, but she wasn't above stirring things up for him by putting ideas into Jenna's head.

Jenna nearly fell off Gold, laughing at the thought of asking her father to buy her a horse trailer. "I can just image his reaction to that suggestion!"

"I've got an idea," James came and joined them. "How about offering a day at the Redchester show as an event for the vacation riders? Then you could do a couple of classes and be working for your dad at the same time. You never know. They might want to compete themselves."

"The boy is a genius," said Sarah, giving James a friendly pat on the shoulder. She liked James, especially the way he looked after Jenna.

"It's a thought. Dad might rent me a truck for the day. I'll ask him tonight!"

Jenna's strategy worked and, in the lounge that evening, Dave went as far as to say he would consider hiring her a trailer for the day.

"Of course, it is possible that your guests…" he consulted his diary, "Mr. Andrews and Miss Bradley, might have room for you in their trailer. You can call them if you like and ask them if they want to enter the show. On second thought, perhaps I'll do it myself. I need to confirm some other details with them."

Jenna was pleased. She was getting more confident with the guests, but she still didn't like getting too involved with the organization of their vacation.

"What time are the guests arriving tomorrow?" James asked her. He had been sitting very quietly in the armchair by the window, and Jenna wasn't sure if he had been listening to the conversation or not.

"Some time after lunch. They said they would call when they were nearly here." She looked at him meditatively. "You seem thoughtful."

"I am thoughtful! Do you want to know what I've been thinking about?" He smiled at her.

"Not really!"

"Well, I'll tell you anyway. I was wondering if you've opened Mr. Penrose's parcel yet." He watched her eyes closely, gauging her reaction to what he knew was a touchy subject.

"No, I came very close to opening it the other morning, but you trying to drown yourself and Sarah's horses getting ill put it out of my mind again. I do feel better about it, though."

"Want to open it now, together?"

There was real note of excitement in James' voice, and Jenna couldn't help herself laughing at him. "You're like a kid at Christmas! All right, let's go and do it now."

They raced up to Jenna's room and she felt under the bed until her hand came across the cold, hard package.

"Here, you open it," she handed it to James who sat on the bed and took his penknife from his pocket.

"It's heavy," he said as he carefully split the taped seals around the old cookie tin and lifted the lid. Jenna felt a chill steal across her shoulders and she wrapped her arms around herself for comfort.

"It's just an old tooth, a whale's, by the look of it. It's got a picture carved into it," James was unable to keep the disappointment from his voice. "And there's a note too."

James cradled the large tooth in his hands and studied it carefully. It was yellowed and grainy with a soft, smooth surface. On one side was a fine drawing of a tall ship, heading full sail across its length and curving into the point. The quality was extraordinary, and James strained his eyes to take in every detail of the rigging. Not Jenna's sort of thing, he thought to himself, and tried hard to image why Mr. Penrose thought she would like it, unless... James stared at the ship's bows. Unless it was the figurehead that he thought might interest her. He turned it over and read out loud the inscription on the other side, which was written in an old-fashioned, fancy script.

"'The Pegasus, Origin of Fairport Harbor, Commanded by John Barker, September 1808'. It's about two hundred years old, wow!"

"The Pegasus? That's what's written on the old decanter on my windowsill," Jenna was surprised.

He handed her the tooth and turned his attention to the note. "*Dear Jenna,*" he read aloud, "*I found this when I was cleaning the spare room and thought it would interest you as it came from the hotel. I was given it as a retirement gift, but my wife never liked it, and it has been in a cupboard for years. It's a whale's tooth, carved by a sailor. I took a shine to it because of its name, the Pegasus, and because of the lovely figurehead. Anyway, it belongs at the hotel and I want you to have it. I shall give this to Sheila tonight when I see her, as I've not been feeling well today. Please bring Tufty to see me soon.*

  Kind regards,
  Samuel Penrose."

When James looked up Jenna was standing by the window staring at the whale tooth through tears that streamed down her face. Oh, not again, he thought, and just when she seemed to be getting back to normal. He went over to her and laid his arm around her shoulder.

"I'm sorry," he said, "I didn't think it would upset you so much."

"I'm not upset," Jenna smiled through her long, wet lashes, "I'm happy! Look," she pointed at the ship, scratched into the surface of the tooth, and at the carved wooden horse, the figurehead, that proudly adorned its magnificent prow. The horse's noble head was set at an angle and its stiff, wooden mane was wind-blown as defiant hooves struck the air. Carved wings, like an angel's, wrapped around the ship's bows.

"That's him," she traced the outline with a tender finger. "We've found the Sand Horse!"

chapter thirteen

The next morning, just after nine thirty, Jenna and James ran
to the village, just in time to board the crowded Redchester
bus and claim the last two seats. James sat next to a tired-
looking woman in a sun hat, and Jenna plunked herself down
beside an old lady with a cane. The old lady sniffed loudly
and looked at her pointedly. Jenna felt self-conscious. She
had gotten up very early to do the mucking out, and in her
haste to be on time for the bus, she had changed her clothes,
but forgotten to wash, and a strong smell of stables was
emanating from her. *I bet I've got straw in my hair too, like
James has*; she looked across at him and blushed at the
thought. *Even with straw in his hair he's good looking*, she
sighed as she watched him sorting through the printed papers
in his folder. The night before, they had gone on to the
Internet and searched for information about the ship, The
Pegasus. It had proved very fruitful, but they had yet to
find a link between her and the Green Horse Hotel, though
it seemed likely that there was one since the tooth and the
decanter both belonged there. They hoped that the local
history section in the Redchester Museum might provide
some help. Jenna had the whale's tooth in a bag on her lap,
and she found its heavy, solid feel reassuring. She knew
that somehow it was the missing link they needed, and she
was confident that the mystery of the Sand Horse would
soon be cleared up. When they reached the granite-gray,

123

town of Redchester, the bus stopped right outside the museum and James took Jenna's hand as they ran up the stone steps together.

"A slave ship?" Jenna gasped, staring open-mouthed at the computer screen. "How horrible!"

Mary Metcalfe, the young research student who was helping them, opened another window on the screen and more information came to light.

"'678 tonnes, schooner rigged, to carry 362 slaves.' She was an English vessel, according to this, and she disappeared in 1809. That was two years after Britain and the USA abolished the slave trade, but of course it still went on for some time after that," Mary smiled at them and sniffed slightly. She was sure she could smell horses.

"Is there any way we can find out about the captain, John Barker?" James asked.

"Possibly. There's a website that has shipping registers and even passenger lists that might help."

"We want to know if he was a local man, and if he had anything to do with my parents' hotel," Jenna explained.

"You could look at local records and newspapers for the time of the ship's disappearance. If he was a local man there might have been a notice in one of them. We have them on microfiche, but it's a pretty laborious job searching through it all," Mary told them.

"I don't mind trying," said James. "I could stay now and do it, Jen. You have to be back by lunchtime to greet the new guests, but you don't need me there."

Jenna smiled at James's eager expression and remembered how much he liked a mystery to solve. He'd been the same when they were researching the plot for the murder weekend at Christmas.

"All right, if you're sure you don't mind me abandoning you," Jenna said.

She caught the next bus back to the village and was walking along the lane to the hotel when she heard the familiar sound of Steve's antique sports car behind her. He stopped for her to get in and she rode the last half-mile in the nearest thing to style that the battered old car could muster.

"Have you got time to help me take some photos of Harry?" Steve asked as they wandered into the stable yard together. "There's a guy in the city who's interested in buying a share in him, and he wants me to e-mail him some pictures."

Jenna checked her watch before saying yes, but it was only pretense as she always had time for Steve.

Steve led the big, bay gelding out of his stable and took a body brush to him while Jenna held his rope. The grooming tickled and Harry lifted a hind foot impatiently, but put it down again quickly after Steve warned him with a growl.

"That'll do. My camera is in the car," Jenna watched Steve's lean frame as he crossed the yard in his long, easy stride and thought how like one of his Thoroughbred horses he was.

"My dad gave me this," he told her as he stared uncomprehendingly at the small silver camera, "but I'm still working out how to use it."

The camera bleeped and beeped cheerfully.

The photo session took longer than it should have, due mostly to the fact that Harry couldn't seem to manage standing tall and square and looking alert and interested all at the same time.

"Typical male," Jenna teased as she pushed him back into position, "he can't do two things at once."

"That's good with the legs. Now make him put his ears forward, Jen."

Jenna found some mints in her pocket and rustled the paper.
"Perfect," Steve shouted. "Now I'll do some head shots."

Steve walked around the big horse taking pictures, but Harry didn't like the noise of the bleeping camera so he tugged at the rope and pulled Jenna round in circles as he snorted. Jenna's face was getting red with effort and Steve thought she looked sweet and couldn't help taking some photos of her too.

"At least he looks alert now," Steve said as he stroked Harry's nose. "Here, have a look."

Jenna took the camera from Steve and scrolled through the images, scowling at the close-up ones of herself, but secretly liking the long shots, which showed off her figure. The sunlight made it hard to view the little screen and Steve, standing behind her, put his arm around her shoulders and cupped his hands over the camera to block out the light. Their closeness was friendly and natural and lasted just a few, precious, fleeting seconds, but Jenna savored every moment of it and wondered if he knew what even so small a gesture of intimacy did to her racing heart.

Later that day Steve downloaded the images on to his father's computer and e-mailed the best ones of Harry to the man in the city. Safely stored on disc, he started erasing them from the memory card in the camera where they disappeared before his eyes, changing into large, blue, pixels. When he came to the ones of Jenna he found he couldn't press the button so he left them in the camera along with the other special shots that he found he liked to look at during the quieter, more wistful moments of his busy life.

Jenna had such a hectic afternoon that it wasn't until she was washing her hands before sitting down to the egg and potato salad that Angie had made her, that she realized that James still wasn't back. She looked at the kitchen clock; it was almost five thirty. Where was he?

"Try his cell phone," Angie suggested, as she put bowls of grated carrot, beetroot and savory rice on the table.

"It's switched off," Jenna told her a few seconds later. "The last bus from Redchester gets into the village about now. Do you mind if I go and… Oh, here he is!"

James breezed into the kitchen carrying a sheaf of papers in one hand and some squashed-looking flowers in the other.

"For you," he gave them to Jenna and kissed her lightly on the cheek, making her blush.

Angie turned away, smiling to herself.

"A fat lady on the bus sat on them," he explained. "I hope they'll expand again when you get them in some water."

"You've been gone forever. I was worried," said Jenna, forgetting to thank him for the gift.

"I know, I'm sorry. The time just flew by. It was fascinating; I got totally absorbed by it all and kept going off on tangents."

"Did you learn anything useful?" Jenna asked as she helped herself to carrot and beetroot.

"I know who John Barker was and I know that he owned the Pegasus at the time it went missing, and best of all, I think I know why the whale's tooth ended up at the Green Horse Hotel."

Dave wandered into the kitchen and sat down at the table. Angie put a plate of hard-boiled eggs in front of him.

"Barker? That rings a bell," Dave said with a puzzled look on his face.

"John Barker bought the hotel at a public auction in August, 1807. He was a successful slave dealer and had made huge amounts of money taking slaves from the west coast of Africa and shipping them to America. The British

Government outlawed the trade during the same year as he bought the hotel, so perhaps he was intending to stop and settle down."

"The slave trade. How horrible," said Angie.

"But we found out that the Pegasus was lost in 1809. That was two years later," Jenna reminded him.

"That's the bit that is rather vague. It seems as though Barker had had enough of owning the hotel and had set off for Africa to trade again. The records say he took glass beads, iron bars…" James shuffled through some photocopies to find the information he was looking for, "linen, calico and pewter, which he stated he was going to trade for spices and sugar, but as Mary pointed out, the slave trade went on illegally for many years after the ban and those things were typical of the goods he would have traded for slaves when it was legal."

"So he might have been going for slaves again," said Angie. She shifted her chair forward to let her husband pass as he rose from his seat and left the room.

"We will never know for certain, but plenty of them did, apparently. The ship's destination was Africa. We know she left Falmouth in July, 1809. There were terrible storms soon after she sailed and several ships were lost, but the Pegasus was never heard of again and her wreck was never found."

"Which means?" asked Jenna.

"Which *might* mean that she was wrecked within a few miles of the coast here and that her figurehead got washed back into the bay at Rush," James said, eyes sparkling with excitement.

"But surely," said Angie, "the figurehead would have been washed away before now."

"It might not if it was still attached to the rest of the ship," said Jenna, "what if the whole of the wreck is lying beneath

128

the sand and on certain tides just the horse's head becomes visible before it's buried again?"

"But if it got so close to the shore, surely it would have been seen and reported," said James, "All the records I could find list her as missing."

"It's possible. Not all wrecks were reported in those days because the locals who found them looted them. It was a regular supplement to their livelihood," said Angie.

Dave came back into the room at that moment, carrying a small and very dusty painting, which he held up to show them. Jenna recognized it immediately as one of the ones from the dining room, but it hung in a dimly lit corner behind the piano and she had never paid it much attention before. Her father handed it to her, and a sharp shock of recognition rocked her forcibly. It was a portrait of a young, black woman who stared out of the painting with very sad, dark eyes.

"I knew I remembered seeing the name Barker," said Dave, "and I was right; look, it says on the back that her name was Constance Barker. I remember seeing it when we had the pictures down for redecorating."

"I always wondered how that painting came to be in the hotel," Angie said. "I hung it at the back of the dining room because it made me sad to look at her. It's a beautiful painting, though."

"I've been reading about the dreadful conditions that the slaves had to endure on the ships," James told them. "The Pegasus was supposed to carry 362, but it often left Africa with over 400 on board because so many of them died during the crossing."

Jenna looked deep into the eyes of the woman from her nightmares and could see only despair and unhappiness there. She blinked back the tears as she imagined her terrifying journey across the seas on the despicable slave ship and considered her life thereafter at the beck and call of those who owned her. She shut her eyes, but the familiar face was still with her. It was as if she could see everything, suddenly clearly through Constance's eyes. She could feel the world shaking alarmingly and she sank to the floor as waves crashed over her, dragging at her, tearing at her. She couldn't breathe and she couldn't move as her arms and legs were held fast, and still the water rose around her. From a very long way away she could hear her name being called, first by her father, then her mother, then by a man's voice that she couldn't put a name to. All she knew was that she loved this man deeply. She had almost been lost, but for him, and only for him, she would make the last effort to return, to save herself from this dreadful, watery grave. The room was spinning uncontrollably when she opened her eyes and saw the anxious faces of Angie, Dave and James as they stood, towering over her.

"Jenna," there was the wonderful voice again. Steve's breath was sweet and familiar as he knelt beside her. She gave him a look that told him everything and he squeezed her hand to say that he felt it too, then he lifted her gently into an armchair.

Jenna shut her eyes again and waited for the dizziness to go. When she opened them again it was just Dave, Angie and James who fussed around her anxiously.

"Where's Steve?" Her own voice sounded distant.

"Steve? I don't know, in the yard I expect. I haven't seen him at all today," her mother's voice was soothing, though her words were confusing.

"He was here," Jenna insisted.

"He wasn't, darling, he *really* wasn't. Now sip this and you'll feel better."

130

"But he lifted me into this chair," she insisted.

"That was me," James came and knelt beside her and gave her a look of complete devotion.

Jenna shut her eyes again. What was real and what was a dream? Sometimes life was just too confusing.

An hour later she was back to normal and sitting in the garden enjoying the last warm rays of the sunny day. James was reading the documents that he'd copied at the museum. He felt her eyes upon him and he leaned over and squeezed Jenna's hand.

"You gave us a terrible shock, fainting like that," he said, looking at her with concern. "Do you think it was heat stroke again?"

"I haven't got a clue what came over me. It was just like being back in those horrible dreams I've been having, except this time I was able to save myself and it didn't all seem quite so hopeless."

"Are you still having them?" James asked, "I didn't realize."

"Not every night, mostly I'm too tired to dream, but when I do it seems that there's always water. Mom thought that the painting of the shipwreck was triggering it, but I'm not sure. This afternoon I just seemed to slip away when I was thinking about the woman in the painting. It was almost as if I became her for a few seconds."

"You are too imaginative for your own good," James told her firmly.

"Maybe," Jenna replied, but she could only say what she thought had happened.

James got up from the deck chair and stretched.

"I'm going to ask your mom if I can borrow her car." James told her, looking at his watch. "There are still a couple of hours of daylight left and I really want to have another

131

look for the Sand Horse. Just from the cliff top, no more boating antics just yet. You stay here if you're too tired."

Jenna thought for a second or two as she watched him walk across the lawn. Then she jumped up and ran after him.

"Wait for me, I'm coming too!" She called after him, as he had known she would.

They parked in the lot next to the closed ice cream stand and walked, hand in hand, to the coast path. When the track became too narrow to walk side by side, James stretched his arm back to Jenna and gripped her fingers, needful of the comfort of her touch. The evening was beautiful and warm as the sun headed for the horizon and flooded the sea with a red-gold flame.

"You are so lucky to live near here," James told her as he looked far out to sea and breathed the distinctive, salty air.

They found the place where Jenna had first seen the Sand Horse and scanned the rippling shallows for the familiar shape.

"Nothing," said James, with disappointment in his voice. "Maybe if we walk down there a little way we might get a better angle. I'm desperate to see if it looks the same as the picture that's carved on the tooth."

He slithered down the slope of the cliff. Jenna watched from above, unsure of what to do. The cliff wasn't steep at that point but she knew that the grassy slope could be unstable at the edges of the path. James reached another path and started to walk in the opposite direction, so she followed him from the higher path and scanned the water's edge.

"There!" James shouted suddenly.

She looked at where he was pointing, but could make out nothing. She scrambled down to the lower path and when she stood beside him the shape of the horse in the shallow waters was suddenly sharply outlined as the last of the sun's rays caught at the elusive carving's battered edges.

"I'm going closer," James set off before she could stop him.

She was just seconds behind him when he reached the water line as it lapped unthreateningly against the foot of the cliff. As the sun moved down they crossed a flat rock to keep the horse in their sight and sat, snuggled into the summer-warmed rock face, until the horse disappeared as completely as if a conjurer had waved his magic wand.

"There is something compelling about it," James said at last, "I can understand why Mr. Penrose went in the water after it. It seems to sort of draw you to it."

"I know... and it's not exactly a nice feeling either," Jenna sensed this strongly now, "there's something sinister about it. I think it's because the Pegasus was a slave ship, and dreadful things happened to the African people when they sailed in her."

"You mean she was a ship constantly filled with pain and sadness and cruelty," James asked her, "and some of the wretchedness somehow stayed with her?"

"Yes, it's like when you go into a building and can feel a horrible atmosphere, and later you're told that someone was murdered there hundreds of years before." Jenna looked out to sea at the setting sun and tried to make sense of all the thoughts that were filling her head.

"It's lovely sitting here, though," James said, putting his arm around her and pulling her closer to him.

She liked it when James did that, but it didn't stop her thinking about Steve. Jenna wondered about herself. What sort of girl was she when she could be the girlfriend of one boy and constantly compare him to another? *Am I in love with James*? She asked herself. *Or am I in love with Steve? Could I be in love with both of them? Maybe there are different kinds of love*, she thought to herself. *James is a very lovable person.* She laid her head against his shoulder, and they watched the sun dip below the line of the sea.

"Better be getting home," James sighed. He didn't want to leave. He'd been enjoying every moment.

He got to his feet and turned in the direction they had come. It was getting chilly now that the sun was down. They must have been sitting there far longer than he'd thought. They retraced their steps across the flat rock, which ended at the cliff base where they had climbed down.

"Oh, no!" James saw the water first, liquid black and rising visibly. Already it had cut them off from their path back up the cliff.

"Should we try to wade through it?" Jenna asked, unable to keep the panic from her voice.

James weighed their chances on the submerged rocks. The swell was getting stronger, and if they slipped they might be swept under the current and bashed against the cliff face.

"Let's try the other way," he said, wanting to sound calm, but he was scared.

They went beyond their resting place; how cold it looked now, not the safe, comforting nest it had been just a few minutes before. They walked a few more yards before they came to a sheer drop into the sea, which now seemed as though it was all around them.

"I feel so stupid. I know to watch the tides, I just didn't think we'd get caught like this," Jenna's voice sounded high and strange with anxiety.

In desperation James looked upwards. The rock was quite sheer and but there were several fault lines and cracks which might make foot holds. He'd been taught climbing at school, but that had been indoors on a specially designed wall with ropes and an instructor guiding his every move. That was a million miles away from this flat, slippery surface with the light fading and the rising water to claim him should he fall.

"There's nothing we can do. We'll have to phone for help," James told her.

"Oh, surely not. Can't we try wading through the water? I don't mind getting wet," Jenna was embarrassed. She should have known to watch the tides. She really didn't want to call the coastguard or the police. That was the sort of thing that vacationers did – not a local like she was. Goodness only knew what her dad would have to say about it.

"Let's have another look." James was doubtful as they crossed the rock again.

The water had risen further and they could only just see the rocks they had scrambled over. A breeze had begun to whip up white froth that spun on the swirling eddies of black water.

"Definitely not," James felt he had to take charge. "I'm going to phone the coastguard. You may want to risk getting swept out to sea, but I'd rather take my chances with a bit of professional help. It's what it's there for."

James took his phone from his jacket pocket and as he looked at the screen a great chill of fear hit him.

"Jen… try yours. Mine has no signal," James walked to the edge of their rocky platform, but there wasn't the least flicker of a signal. "Jenna, get your phone out and try it." Fear made James's voice sharp.

"I haven't got it with me," Jenna whispered. "What do we do now?"

There was a long silence before James replied.

"We shout," he told her, "We shout and scream for all we're worth and just pray that someone hears us."

Frank Harris was angry. His wife's black Labrador, Bouncer,

had run off on the scent of a rabbit, and no amount of calling would bring him back. Frank trudged back up the path and shouted again. He could see the wretched dog with its head down a hole, not taking the least bit of notice of his master, as usual. Frank was standing with his back to the sea when he first thought he heard something. The wind was getting stronger and, despite the failing daylight, there were still several gulls riding on the air currents. Frank heard it again. That wasn't gulls. That was someone shouting for help. His heart started racing as, errant dog forgotten, he ran to the cliff edge and looked over. His head for heights was poor and he immediately felt dizziness flood through him, but the cries were unmistakably human now, though he couldn't see anyone.

"Hello," he cried into the gloomy dusk.

"Stuck," was the only word he could make out for sure, so he took out his cell phone and punched in 911, the emergency service's number.

It was cold, very, very cold at the water's edge. Dark too. And more worrying, it was becoming wet on the rock as the sea level rose and lapped over the edge. The table-like rock was still dry for two or three yards around them, but Jenna knew that the water would reach them soon and then the cold, combined with the wet, would become insufferable. And what if help didn't come? Jenna couldn't bear to think about that.

"I'm beginning to think we weren't heard after all," James confessed. The light from his watch dial told him that they had been on the rock for almost an hour. He had gladly and gallantly given Jenna his hooded sweatshirt, but was now shivering in his tee shirt as they clung together for warmth.

"Even if we weren't, Mom and Dad will be worried by now

and probably be out looking for us," Jenna sounded more positive than she felt. She knew that in reality her Dad would be busy in the bar and that her mom was probably just about to serve coffee in the dining room. Their darling daughter, precious as she undoubtedly was to them, was out with James; sensible James, who could be trusted to look after her.

"Jen?" The darkness and the extreme gravity of their situation made James suddenly bold. There was something he had needed to know for some time and he didn't want to die with the question still unanswered.

"Yes."

"Do you love me?"

It was a fair question and Jenna had sensed it was coming. Normally it would have elicited a quick, lightly positive reply, but now, with the enormity of their predicament becoming clear to them both, Jenna felt she had to answer properly. She searched her heart for the truth. Yes, she loved him as a friend, yes, she loved his company, yes, she thought him handsome and kind and she liked the way that other girls seemed envious of her when they were out together. If her cherished feelings for Steve hadn't led her to suspect that there was something else, a deeper, more precious layer to the strange make-up of love, then perhaps she might have thought that she loved him unquestionably. But she suspected there was more to it. Something magical, when the merest touch could send a thrill through your body like an electric shock, and a single glance could communicate volumes and volumes of unspoken words. The person who you shared this with knew what you were thinking before you'd even thought it and understood you totally, instinctively and without question.

"I… I do love you…" she said at last, "but I don't think I'm in love with you. I... I don't think I love you in the way that you love me."

137

It sounded starkly honest but it was the best way she had to describe her feelings. She felt the grip on her hand lessen and then drop completely, though the arm around her shoulder remained firm and warm and kindly. A strange fear crept into Jenna's heart. Had she said too much? Had her honesty lost him forever? She was surprised to feel tears pricking the backs of her eyes – after all she had just said, why did she care so much?

"I thought so," James said sadly, "It's Steve, isn't it? You're in love with him, aren't you?"

"I'm not sure…" Jenna didn't want to talk about Steve with James, and she honestly found the complexities of her feelings for him baffling and unformed. But it was time for being honest, with herself as much as anyone. Jenna thought back to the strange incident when she'd fainted. She'd felt feelings of love that were so strong she'd assumed it must be Steve, but in reality it had been James.

"Perhaps I'm just in love with the *thought* of Steve." It was an interesting idea and it seemed to make sense to Jenna. "Anyway, he's not in love with me, and he's much older. It would be an impossible relationship."

"Now perhaps, but not in a few years," James wondered why he was encouraging her. Perhaps it revealed the depth of his feelings for her, that he wanted her to be happy, whatever the consequences might be for him.

Jenna shook her head sadly in the darkness. She'd never talked to anyone about her feelings for Steve before, never formed them so coherently in her head and put them into words. In the dark, on the rocks with the inky black sea creeping threateningly toward them, Jenna realized for the first time the importance of living in the present time and not wistfully yearning for something that isn't really there. Suddenly it was clear to her that what she had with Steve was just a schoolgirl crush on an older man, not the sort of joyful, youthful partnership that she could have with James.

"James...I don't want to spoil 'now' for something that might never happen in the future. I *do* love you and I... I *am* in love with you," she whispered the words and wasn't sure if he'd heard her, but he had.

"It *is* all about now, Jen. It's all we ever really have," he took her hand again and a magical surge of electricity passed between them.

The trouble is that now we're dangerously alone, he thought to himself, *and this might be the end for both us. Did she really just tell me that she isn't in love with me, and in the next breath seem to be saying the very opposite?* James's head was throbbing and his heart was filled with strange, unasked-for emotions, and fear of the night which was so black and terrifying, full of noises and...

"James, can you hear something?"

"No, what?"

"Listen... it's a helicopter, I'm sure it's a helicopter. It must be coming for us."

Suddenly a strong beam of light flashed over the cliffs and a man's voice, distorted by a loud megaphone, shouted down to them.

"Is anyone there?"

Together James and Jenna jumped up and shouted as loudly as they could.

"We'll be with you soon. Stay where you are," the voice replied.

There were lights and a scraping, scrambling noise from above.

"Someone's coming down the cliff," James cried, relief flooding through him in torrents.

The water was over their shoes now and they clung together

and tried to keep back their tears. The downdraft from the helicopter flattened the sea and tore at their hair and clothes, but the air was strangely warm and the searchlights bathed them in a harsh, white glow. It lifted their spirits.

"Tell me again that you love me now," James had to shout now as the noise of the blades was deafening. "Because I'm always going to love you 'now'... now and forever, you can't stop me!"

Something stirred inside Jenna, a thrill of pure emotion seemed to burst from her as his words sunk in. Despite everything she had said, she hadn't lost him.

"You are the nicest person I have ever met," she told him, "and I love you… *really* love you. I think I probably always have."

He smiled down at her and she smiled back, a broad, loving, happy grin that lit up her beautiful, tear-stained face and tore at his tortured heart.

chapter fourteen

Nothing that girl ever does again will surprise me, Dave Wells thought to himself as he opened the mail very early the next morning. He was tired, having had an exciting, disturbing night. It was the sort of excitement he could do without at his age. Jenna and James had arrived back after dark in a police car, wet and cold and strangely euphoric considering the trouble they had put everyone to. It had caused a few raised eyebrows among the late night diners in the restaurant, and he still hadn't heard the full story because Angie had insisted on baths, hot drinks and bed for the exhausted pair. No doubt someone would fill him in later.

He was putting a pile of catalogues and envelopes into the recycling bag when the unbearable thought suddenly hit him. Jenna might have been killed last night. His beautiful, precious child had been out on the cliffs and he hadn't known about it. He had been too busy at the beck and call of other people, customers and guests; strangers for whom he cared nothing. Tears welled at the back of his eyes and he brushed his hand across his cheek. It was his fault and he was going to have to do something about it. The hotel was their livelihood, but it shouldn't be their ball and chain. There were other things that were just as important, and Dave was determined to make some time for them. In many ways he didn't really know Jenna. He'd never even seen her ride Gold at a horse show, and she was pretty good by all accounts. Dave made some firm resolutions as he pulled himself together. The sun broke through a cloud and streamed through the office window, falling warmly on to his face.

"She's all right! Thank goodness," he said aloud.

Breakfast was late and eaten slowly by Jenna and James. Steve had offered to take the riding guests out for the day and Dave put his first resolution into practice and stopped what he was doing to sit and chat with his daughter.

"Everyone is being very kind," Jenna said. "We expected to be yelled at for being so stupid."

"Part of me wants to," admitted Angie, "but not a very big part. Dave and I are just so relieved that you're both all right."

"I'm *really* sorry, Mr. Wells," James found it hard to meet Dave's gaze, "I should have looked after her better."

"It's funny you should say that, James, because I was accusing myself of the very same thing this morning." Dave told him wryly.

"Phone's ringing, honey," Angie told her husband.

"When isn't it? Ange, we'll just *have* to get a receptionist… or a manager… or another business…" he continued, muttering to himself as he left the room.

"He doesn't mean it, does he? About getting another business?" Jenna was anxious. Although hotel life was sometimes difficult, she loved the place and couldn't bear the idea of leaving.

Angie shrugged, "I don't suppose he does, though I'm sure we could afford to have some extra help now. The profits are pretty healthy at the moment. More toast?"

They talked about the rescue, and Jenna described the feeling of being winched to safety, hovering above the water, too terrified to look down, yet too scared to close her eyes.

142

"The man I was strapped to just asked me questions, really crazy ones like what my favorite color was and which bands I like," Jenna remembered. "It was weird, I just answered him and before I knew it I was inside the helicopter and being wrapped in a blanket."

"That was Paul, he was really nice," said James, "I was telling him about the Sand Horse when we got back and he was very interested. He's a history buff, apparently."

Dave came back into the kitchen with a big smile on his face.

"I don't know, you two!"

"What?" James and Jenna chorused together.

"You do seem to land on your feet, thank goodness!"

"What's happened?" Angie was intrigued by her husband's complete change of countenance.

"That call was from a Mr. Ford, Mr. Paul Ford. He was one of the men who rescued you last night. He's very excited about your Sand Horse; he agrees that it could be part of the wreck of the Pegasus and he wants to take you both up in the helicopter again so that he can try to locate it. Then he'll organize a dive to see what they can find out."

"There might be treasure," said Angie, letting her imagination get the better of her common sense.

"On a slave ship? I doubt it, though knowing the luck of this pair it's probably full of gold bars. Up in a helicopter again! I don't know," he chuckled as he went back to his work.

In the days that followed, things started to happen very fast for the Sand Horse, which had lain almost unnoticed on the seabed for over two hundred years. First he was located from the air, using sophisticated depth-indicating technology, then he was thoroughly mapped and charted, photographed and documented, until finally, on a cold September morning, with the press of the nation there to watch, he was carefully lifted from his deep, sandy grave, along with most of what remained of the hull of the Pegasus. Unstable in the air, he was rushed in seawater tanks to the laboratories of the National Maritime Museum where he endured detailed and exhaustive processes to stabilize his delicate state. Finally, many months later, he went on display, taking center stage among the museum's collection of figureheads. Away from his ship and separated from his past connections, he could at last be admired for what he was – a magnificent, wooden horse. Jenna visited him sometimes and wondered why she had been afraid.

In the wake of the huge press interest after the wreck had been officially confirmed as the slave ship, Pegasus, Jenna and James hunted through the hotel for other references to the seafaring, former landlord, John Barker. There were now many experts on hand to offer advice and opinions, and the hotel was overrun with journalists, scientists, historians and interested members of the general public. The picture of the wrecked ship that had seemed to haunt Jenna in room three turned out to have been painted at least a hundred years after John Barker had died, but the whale's tooth was valuable and Jenna learned that the art form was called scrimshaw and highly collectible.

"Not that I want to sell it," she explained to an elderly guest who had asked to see the tooth. "It was given to me by a very special friend, you see, but he's dead now." The words didn't hurt her any more.

The glass decanter that stood on Jenna's windowsill was confirmed as belonging to the Pegasus. Its heavy-bottomed shape was typical of nautical artifacts that needed a low center of gravity to stop them toppling over during rough voyages. Mary Metcalf, from the museum, visited the hotel one morning when Jenna was riding and showed James pictures of other glass bottles that had been designed for life on board ship.

"Are they usually decorated with beads?" James asked, running his fingers over the smooth, colorful spheres.

"No, they aren't part of the decanter at all," Mary assured him. "Those are Venetian glass beads, typical of the kind that were used as barter at the time. They were probably worn by someone as a necklace. See, they're threaded on a leather thong, and look, it's about the right size for a slender neck, perhaps a child's neck?"

Mary unwound the string of beads from around the top of the decanter and held them up to the light, which penetrated the deep, dark glass and made them glow with intense, rich colors. It rang a small bell in the depths of James's memory, and he looked thoughtfully at them for some time before he remembered where he had seen them before. Running through the hall to the dining room he almost collided with Dave.

"Where's the fire?" Dave followed him more slowly.

But James wasn't listening. He was standing in front of the painting of Constance Barker with a broad smile on his face.

"Look at them," he demanded of the older man, as he pointed at the portrait, "Constance is wearing the beads from the decanter; they must have belonged to her."

A certificate held at the museum confirmed that Constance had married John Barker in August, 1807.

"Which must have been very controversial, at the time," Paul Ford, who had become a frequent visitor to the hotel, told them. "She was a native of Africa, and a freed slave, but to marry the Captain of a slave ship was extraordinary."

145

"She was only married for two years before John's ship was lost." James felt so sad for this woman who he felt strangely close to, despite their lives being separated by nearly two hundred years.

Documents, found in one of the hotel attics, suggested that John Barker's widow had lived on at the Green Horse Inn, and managed the business after the Pegasus was lost.

"This was most unusual, because at the beginning of the nineteenth century women were rarely in a position to own their own businesses. For a black woman, who had also been a slave, well, this was practically unheard of," said Paul.

History at school was never this interesting or this real, thought James as he listened.

"Does that mean that John Barker was a good man at heart, if he married a black woman and set her free?" Jenna asked, unable to quite imagine a world where people were owned.

Paul thought about this for a while before he answered. "Maybe there was some good in him if he fell in love with Constance and had the courage to make her his wife; in those days it wouldn't be the straightest path to social acceptance! But you can't forgive him his trade however hard you try; it was the most appalling way to make money."

It was James who made the most significant discovery about the sad life of Constance Barker. He had searched without success for her grave in the local churchyard, and he had gone to the museum to search through their records again, when he found the entry in a newspaper, which seemed to be the key to all their questions. He wanted to tell Jenna himself, so he waited until she had fed the horses for the night and sat her down on an upturned bucket in the yard.

"I know why Constance isn't buried in the churchyard.

146

Look, I've found this." He handed her the photocopy and she read the few words that explained so much to them.

With tears in her eyes Jenna looked up.

"So she took her own life?"

"Yes, she threw herself into the sea when she was sure that John wasn't ever going to be coming home to her. At that time, maybe even now, if you took your own life, you couldn't be buried in consecrated ground. If she *is* in the churchyard, her grave was never marked."

"She drowned." It was a flat statement and revealed nothing of the turmoil of feelings that was racing through Jenna's head. Fragments of the dreams came back to her, and when she shut her eyes she could almost feel the salty water and the rush of bubbles dragging her down. Then something came into her mind, something she found she was very sure of.

"She wants her beads back."

"We'll never find the grave."

"Her spirit is in the sea, so that's where we'll put them."

As the summer turned into autumn, Jenna's existence seemed to take a slower turn. True to his word, Dave made changes to the Wells's family life, and this included the hiring of an assistant manager who was being groomed to take charge when Dave took time off with his family. On Sunday and Monday evenings in the restaurant, dinner was prepared by a new, part-time chef who eased Angie's workload considerably; though she wasn't at all sure she liked the feeling of being redundant in her own kitchen. Sarah was persuaded to take over the organization of the riding guests, and courses were to be offered in show jumping and dressage, using her facilities. For this she would get a good share of the profits. Roughly once every hour panic would overtake Dave's new, laid-back approach to life and he would ask himself, "Can we

147

afford it?" But he realized that it wasn't just about making money, and so he would take a deep breath and make himself look forward to spending more time with Jenna and Angie.

The day of the Redchester Show started with an unpromising shower of rain.

"It will soften the ring," James reassured Jenna as she packed the extra large studs in her grooming kit. "Gold likes the ground to have a bit of give in it."

Jenna wasn't talking to anyone. Nerves always got to her in this way and made her retreat into her own, intensely focused, but jittery, world, until the competition was over. The trailer that Dave had hired for the day arrived in the yard at the same time as Sarah, who was taking the riding guests for a daylong trail ride with lunch at a diner.

Gold stepped out nervously, his head and tail held high and his stride exaggerated because of the strange feeling of the protective boots on his legs. He walked up the ramp and a thrill shot through his body as he wondered if he was going racing, as he had in the days before Jenna had bought him. James was going with her, but Steve had tactfully declined, feigning a prior appointment, and he had been touched and a little saddened when he had noticed the fleeting look of relief that had passed over the younger man's face at this news. He wished Jenna luck and tousled her hair in a big-brotherly sort of way and leaned thoughtfully on his broom as he watched the trailer leaving the yard. Steve took a crumpled letter from his pocket and read it again, though he had read it so many times that he almost knew it by heart. It was from a friend of his father offering him a job as a trainer at his stables in France. It was a fantastic opportunity, a great adventure, a chance to learn and grow and improve, and the money was good, too. So, why wasn't he jumping at it? Why was he so desperate to hang on at the Green Horse yard, where he was running his horses on a shoestring budget and still relying heavily on his father? He knew he couldn't carry on there much longer. He knew that he had to accept the offer. What he didn't know was how and when he was going to tell Jenna.

Dave Wells hardly recognized the confident, beautiful young woman who rode neatly into the ring on her smartly turned-out chestnut horse. He gasped when he saw the height of the jumps she was riding toward, and clenched his fists so tightly that his nails dug deep into the palms of his hands and left red marks there for the rest of the day. His spontaneous cheer was incongruous amongst the polite clapping from the small crowd as Jenna and Gold cleared the last fence to win the class.

"Was that really our daughter?" he asked his laughing wife.

"It was! She's pretty good, isn't she?"

"Good? Good? She's marvelous! Why didn't anyone tell me?"

"We tried to," James told him, "but you were always too busy."

One Sunday morning, in the early autumn, Jenna, James, Dave and Angie drove to Rush Bay. The mood in the car was high and Jenna was trying to persuade her father to buy her a trailer.

"The Hotel could sponsor me," she told him. "It would be terrific advertising for you."

"Who's going to drive it? I know I've said I'll have more time off, but I can't be wandering around the countryside every weekend. And, before you say James will, don't forget he's off to college in a couple of weeks."

James sat silently, smiling to himself and wondering when he might let slip the news that he had deferred his college place for a year.

"There's always Mom, and Steve might when she's too busy," Jenna said, feeling invincible after her success at Redchester. She had been used to doing well, but to have the active support and approval of her father was a new and heady feeling for her.

"We'll see," was Dave's tantalizing reply, which pleased Jenna hugely – he hadn't actually said no!

The tide was high and a chill breeze buffeted the seagulls as the four of them made their way along the footpath to the cliff edge. They gazed down to the black water where the Pegasus had lain for so many years and they all thought about the strange, sad horse of the sea.

The gulls cried loudly and James, Angie and Dave said a few private, silent words to Constance Barker as Jenna stood tall on the cliff top and flung the glass beads as far as she could across the wind-whipped ocean.

Jenna closed her eyes and saw the face of Constance as she was in her portrait. She saw the sorrow that was so clearly communicated through her sad, dark eyes, but then a warm and magical feeling spread through her as she saw a smile cross the woman's lips.

"No more dreams," Jenna pleaded.

"Only good ones," the wind seemed to answer her back.